The Expert System's Champion

ALSO BY ADRIAN TCHAIKOVSKY

Guns of the Dawn
Dogs of War
Spiderlight
Ironclads
Cage of Souls
Walking to Aldebaran
Firewalkers
The Doors of Eden
Made Things

THE CHILDREN OF TIME
Children of Time
Children of Ruin

ECHOES OF THE FALL
The Tiger and the Wolf
The Bear and the Serpent
The Hyena and the Hawk

THE
EXPERT SYSTEM'S
CHAMPION

A D R I A N   T C H A I K O V S K Y

A TOM DOHERTY ASSOCIATES BOOK

NEW YORK

THE EXPERT SYSTEM'S CHAMPION

Copyright © 2020 by Adrian Tchaikovsky

Cover art by Raphael Lacoste
Cover design by Christine Foltzer

Edited by Lee Harris

A Tordotcom Book
Published by Tom Doherty Associates
120 Broadway
New York, NY 10271

www.tor.com

Tor® is a registered trademark of
Macmillan Publishing Group, LLC.

ISBN 978-1-250-76638-0 (ebook)
ISBN 978-1-250-76639-7 (trade paperback)

First Edition: January 2021

For Alex

Prologue

The Sister Colony: Part One

SEVENTY-TWO HOURS AWAKE and Bain wanted to crash. Lena Dal came in just as the drugs were wearing off, complaining about the sampling drones. "Gone! Another one gone!"

He lay there in his pod. *Just another five minutes.* Except it wouldn't be five minutes. Five hours, five days. It felt as though he could sleep five weeks and still not iron the kinks out. But there weren't enough shoulders to share the load of the new colony. Everyone was pharma'd to the eyeballs to keep them going. It started because the days here were two hours too short, to go with the years being eighty of those days too long. Two hours short; you'd think it would be easy enough to adapt to, but nobody had. *Give me a thirty-six-hour cycle and I reckon I could have lived with it,* Bain told himself, but just two hours too few in the day . . . He'd never settled. And now Lena came stomping in, banging on his lid, just as he was about to have himself put under. "I know you're not gone yet. Bain, we have to talk."

Half an hour later and he was back on the fizzy cocktail that kept them going there, all twenty-eight of them doing the work of fifty people, trying to keep the sister expedition going with practically zero support from the ship. He was back in the ready room of the main dome, out on the shore of an alien sea. Seven of the others were sleeping, lucky them. The rest were in the various lab modules fighting the toxic biochemistry of the planet, trying to find a way to square the circle with poor, abused Earth biology. And then there was Lena, and him.

"We can't get anywhere without samples." Because when Lena said, *We need to talk,* she meant she needed to talk, to tell Bain what they all knew. "I can't get samples if the damn things keep eating my drones. I need escorts. Armed escorts. Drive off the locals."

"Don't call them locals." Bain's voice sounded like it had died, just a raspy croak. "Just one particularly aggressive species. Which is why I don't want to risk—"

"They're just molluscs, Bain."

"They're not molluscs, they just look like—"

"A few of us in environment suits, with guns."

"You're volunteering, are you?" Too tired to be politic.

"Yes, I am," Lena confirmed. "I will personally go out there with a hammer and crack open the next shellfish to try anything. Bain, we are . . . besieged."

"You're being—"

"There are dozens of the things within our immediate area!"

He felt sick. Not at the thought of marauding not-molluscs, because even though they had a taste for drones, for some inexplicable reason, it wasn't as though the lumbering things had proved a *threat*, really. Sick because of the decisions hanging over him that he'd been resolutely refusing to make.

"I think we need to move site," he said weakly, knowing what her response would be.

"No! Bain, the coast is the only place where we've found any give in the biology! You've seen the reports from the ship. It's all poison out there, utterly incompatible with Earth life. But the saltwater biomes, they're flexible. There's a convergence there."

"There are giant molluscs that eat our samplers." He waited for her to parrot his own *not molluscs* back at him, but she didn't. Abruptly half the fight had gone from her and she was looking away, to where the curved side of the dome met the hard plastic of the floor.

"They don't eat them," she said. Innocent enough except there was a big indigestible lump of words she wasn't quite vomiting up. Under the circumstances, and because he was so strung he couldn't think, he just let the silence hang.

"They . . ." And she was just as worn down by the long shifts and the drugs. *We can't keep going. We should abandon this doomed venture and go back to the ship.* Except Bain had heard what sort of measures the lead science team over there were considering and . . . unthinkable. Just unthinkable. *There must be another way, a path that preserves us as human.*

He realised he was crying. He couldn't stop it, and it didn't even engage with him consciously. It was just something his body was doing. Lena looked on dully. *We did all the groundwork,* some scientist part of him was wailing, outraged at an unfair universe. They had known there was a biosphere here they could work with, all the right elements. Oxygen, carbon, plenty of water. *Life,* recognisably the building blocks of life. It was supposed to be paradise, ripe for colonising. Except apparently you could have every familiar Earth element and put them together in a way utterly inimical to anything from Earth. The world rejected them from their arrival, and continued to do so, moment by moment. They couldn't eat it without being poisoned. They couldn't touch it without potentially fatal allergic reactions to *everything.* And they were *here,* now. It wasn't a return trip. Hundreds of would-be colonists, come light years from home, just to plant a flag in a planet that murdered them by its very nature.

"Fine," he spat out, because right then agreeing was less effort. "Guns. Print out guns, ammunition. Something heavy enough to get through those shells." They were the size of a two-person transport, those not-molluscs. Small-arms fire or light energy weapons wouldn't stand a chance. "Or a hammer, if you really want." *And what can they do, poor dumb beasts that they are?* They were the Galapagos tortoises of an alien world, and they wouldn't even have the wit to rue the day they met humanity.

Only after she'd gone, after he was back in his pod with strict instructions to shoot him full of downers and let him sleep for a week, did he realise he never asked her what they did with the sampler drones. What they did, instead of eating, that so discomfited her. But it was too late then, and by the time they woke him, it was a moot point.

~

They were an unlovely thing, Lena Dal thought. But if they'd stuck to simply crawling about in the mud like the snails they resembled, she would have been content to share a world with them. At least until a solution was found to long-term human habitation here. If that solution involved snail genocide she wouldn't weep. She might be a bioengineer but that didn't mean she was soft on every creature in the cosmos.

She'd come out with Shay Park and Orindo Snapper, geologist and technician respectively. They'd used too many expedition resources fabricating large-bore percussion weapons and now they were escorting a sampler drone out along the beach. They'd already seen a dozen of the monstrous mollusc-alikes, even on the short walk from the dome complex to the sea. The sister colony expedition had set up in the wind-shadow of a great rise, a slanted boulder, fifteen metres high, that had been rolled up to the high-water mark by some ancient storm. Or perhaps left by retreating glaciation, though they'd seen little other sign of that. It remained the landscape's lone muck-and-vegetation-encrusted shelter. A bastion against the fierce winds that came off the great greenish expanse of the sea, the water murky as a weed-choked pond with a scum of plankton. Filthy. She wouldn't want to put a foot in it. Yet this ecosystem was the most amenable to conversion for human uses. Coming about the boulder-hill's broad, rounded base, she felt her heart sink at the sight. The beach was utterly desolate, windswept, with a strand line of decaying purple detritus speckled with the odd corpse of some oceanic denizen. Not fish. Not even not-fish as the snails were not-snails. Macrofauna on this world had a kind of a skeleton but no spine. The hydrodynamic shape that evolved over and over on Earth never found a foothold here. Everything that swam was all webbed legs, like spider-crabs crossed with bats. And dead, if it had washed up here. If she weren't suited up, she'd have a noseful of alien decay, a weirdly floral, cloying scent, but a stink, nonetheless. She reckoned they'd stink alive, too. She hated them, but not as much as the snails.

They dominated the beach. She could see thirty of them, the smallest as large as she was, the largest four times that. They made their desultory way along the strand, picking over the detritus. Too big, too slow, too *wrong*. And they didn't care about her. She meant nothing to their creeping existence. Except they didn't even slide about like real snails. Beneath that crumpled, swept-back cone of a shell there were greyish legs, like fingers. As though the snail was a hand nestled into that great stony shell like an obscene hermit crab. Mostly they stayed low, and only the stumps of their fingertips were visible, broad about as Lena's thigh. But she'd seen them move. She'd seen the bastards hustle, from a standing start and without any obvious cause. They lifted their huge shells like ponderous matrons with their skirts, and those grotesque flesh limbs scuttled them along, far too fast for so huge a bulk. The sight had made her ill, when they showed her the footage. She'd hated them ever since.

But she didn't indulge herself. She just escorted the wheeled drone as it motored over to the strand line and began selecting another round of samples from the recently beached. Back at the dome, the expedition scientists, Lena included, would do their level best to find levers amongst this alien biochemistry, to find a way to yoke it to their service. *Or clear it,* said the quiet voice in the back of her mind. Exterminate it, just locally. Just to give them a foothold. *We came so far.*

Like Bain, she'd spoken to their counterparts at the ship. People were dying. The planet was killing them. All attempts at agriculture were stillborn. People were desperate. But Lena Dal told herself that she thrived under pressure. It made her stronger. She fought back.

The sampler drones: she didn't know what it was about the things, but the snails loved them. The expedition team had tried painting them different colours, modulating the engine frequency, signals, emissions. The monsters couldn't resist, no matter what. They came and dismantled them, devoured parts. Not all, but only some components. Mechanisms, the computer brain, certain instruments. As though they were gourmets. She'd seen footage of that, too. The snails were hands within hands, unfolding rubbery mouthparts that were just rings of fingers over smaller fingers until the bile almost choked her.

"Incoming," Shay said and, true to form, the closest snails had started ambling over. When they stayed low, she could almost kid herself that they were just molluscs.

"Do we, what? Give them a warning?" Orindo asked.

"Sure, go tack an eviction notice on 'em," Lena snapped. Loud noises had been tried. No point in a warning shot. She looked around to see where the rest of the things were, because she didn't want to get mobbed, pawed at by those horrible, unformed hands. The rest of the beachcomber population were scattered all the way down the strand line. Safe enough.

She levelled the gun and shot. Recoil compensation meant little of the kinetic kickback got to her shoulder. The snail rocked, and she saw cracks craze the whorled, stony curve of its shell. For a moment it was still, but then it just continued its dogged progress towards the sampler, intent on vandalism.

"I hope the others are capable of learning from this," she said, and gave it another round. The superdense plastic projectile struck close on the crack and a great shard of shell was abruptly hanging away, still attached by sticky membranes and grey flesh to the thing beneath. *Now* the bastard stopped. Now it shuddered and its unspeakable finger-legs drummed and clawed the gritty beach. Without being told, Shay and Orindo did the same to the second, three shots sufficing to shatter its defences and leave it split open and quivering.

They were hollow, she saw. The first one had a mess of organic detritus inside it. The second . . .

Sampler parts. She stared. They'd been there a while, weirdly patinaed, layered over as though becoming outsize alien pearls. For a moment, until she put another round into the mess, until she convinced herself otherwise and recast the memories a different way, she thought there had been an organisation to the pieces. As though the insensate brute had filed them away according to some plan.

~

Bain woke to find the world shaking. The lid of his pod had popped open, evacuation protocols in full swing. Uncontrollable spasms racked his limbs under the chemical onslaught of the emergency wake-up procedure.

He jackknifed up, almost fell face-first out onto the floor. There were klaxons going, panicked voices. He heard gunfire.

"What . . . ? What . . . ?" Croaking pitifully, alone in the sleep room. Above him, the curved ceiling shuddered.

Still wearing just a medical smock, he stumbled out

into a corridor, almost going under the feet of three of his crew. He clawed at them. "What . . . ? What . . . ?" *I'm the director. You have to tell me.*

Two of them just charged off. The third, unable to shake him off, stared wild-eyed. "We have to get out!"

"What is it?" As though, if he got three sentences of briefing, he could magically make it all go away, quell the earthquake, repel the invasion.

"Bain!"

He jerked as his name was called, and the man he had hold of writhed out of his grip and ran. Turning, he saw Lena. She looked . . . She had a gun and there was blood on her, the sleeve of her exosuit torn up.

"We're under attack, Bain," she barked. "Get to the flier."

"Attack?" For a moment his mind just went into free fall. Attack from the other colonists? The planet? The sound of tortured metal from nearby shocked him out of it.

"We need to get you in a suit!" Lena shouted at him. "Come on!"

Behind her, the wall of the corridor deformed, something blunt shunting determinedly against it. There was a lab on the other side of that, and he had sudden thoughts of something grown there, some experiment gone wild . . .

Lena had seen it, too. "They're inside already," she told him, hauling him away. "So we need to get out. Out and away, back to the ship. This was a mistake. It was all a mistake." Up to and including coming to colonise this planet in the first place, her tone said.

"They?" Echoing her was all he could do.

"The snails!"

Impossible. But even as he thought it, even as Lena dragged him off, he saw the corridor wall split behind them, the round, ridgy prow of a shell push through it, dragged forwards on those ghoulish grey fingers.

They got to the airlock, and Lena insisted on him suiting up. Even though her own suit was torn open, her blood exposed to every alien particle that her body would so violently reject. Even though someone had jammed the airlock doors open so people could flee. That brought it home; that made it real. *We're abandoning the expedition.* The whole base was contaminated by the planet, now. They'd start to sicken, soon.

If the snails don't get us.

The flier was ahead. He saw people thronging there. One of the servitors, a nine-foot humanoid form of titanium and plastic, was patiently loading it with crates under Orindo Snapper's direction.

"I've got him!" Lena was yelling. Her voice came dully to Bain through his helmet. "Just get on board! Just—!"

The snail came at them with maniac speed, surely a ton of shell and mushy body, but it was riding high, its rubbery hand of a body at full extension. People threw themselves aside and the servitor was caught by the edge of the shell, flipped end over end with a squeal of complaining electronics.

The sound of the creature ramming the flier was weirdly flat. It didn't sound like the end of the world at all. If Lena had rapped on his faceplate, the noise would have been sharper, more alarming. And yet the machine folded, all those high-strength, hollow components just crumpling before the snail's unstoppable momentum. People were running. People were fleeing in all directions. He heard shots. One thundered from close by as Lena sent a round into that shell, marking it with a jagged white scar.

The creature crouched in the ruin of their flier, their single transport, the only way they could get back to the ship. Its shell cocked and tilted, the rubbery legs beneath lifting it high as though it was exalting. It extruded a mass of prying fingers and began to tear into the ruined machine's innards. He heard Lena scream at it in fear and frustration.

The ground shook again. He'd written it off as the structure of the base under assault, but he was out of the dome now. The ground was just the ground.

Lena was pulling at his arm, but he just turned back to see. No amount of warning could have prevented him.

The hill, the shielding boulder they'd built against, it was moving. Weed and mud at its base bulged and split as it levered itself up. He saw the vast limbs there, like the hand of a half-formed god.

I

AS WE MADE OUR way through the last of the trees towards Meravo, the children saw us. I think the adults sent them out that way, their scouts having had sight of us for a while. The little ones didn't know what was going on, and we heard their shrieking as they spotted us between the bristling, feathery trunks. An odd sound; part terror, part excitement. Half of them were too young to remember us the last time we came this way, but they heard stories. Children are their own secret Order, with their own initiations, legends and rites. The thought made our business seem innocent by association.

"The Bandage-Men!" they cried, and fled ahead of us. "Don't let them get you!" And I knew their parents must tell them: be good, do your share, or the Bandage-Men will claim you.

And it was true. We would.

We'd become a part of their world in just ten years, which before us had nothing new in it for many centuries, and that gives me hope. Things can change, which mean they can get better.

Those children saw us as dread figures, terrors to scare them into being good. We were the Bandage-Men and they told each other tales about what lay beneath our wrappings, what wounds, what decay and deformity. Were we even alive, or just corpses, skeletons, beasts pretending to human shape? They could never know that when we take someone away to become part of our bandaged brotherhood, it is a mercy. It is better than the alternative.

My name is Handry and I am many things.

To my home village of Aro, which I have not seen for many, many years, I was an outcast. Cut off from the rest of humanity after being daubed with the Severance, that mystical potion the doctor ghosts concoct, when someone *has* been so bad that the village can no longer support them. Severed, you become no longer one of *us*, no longer a part of the world. All men's hands turned against you, all the fruits of the world poison in your mouth. And then, as it used to be, you die.

To Sharskin the priest, who found me after my Severance, who took me to the House of our Ancestors, I was a human of the Original Condition. He taught me that what had been Severed from me was not my birthright, but an addition, an adaptation. He said what I was now, despised, rejected, was nonetheless the native state of a human being. And, although he was wrong about so many things, in this he was correct.

And he has been dead for many, many years, too, but sometimes I hear his voice still. In my head, mostly, though occasionally the ancestors remember it and use it in their House to speak to me.

To the other Bandage-Men, I am their leader, the new priest of the new doctrine, who came after Sharskin. And to them, we are not the Bandage-Men of the children's nightmares, but the Order of Cain. Simultaneously outcast and elevated, despised and necessary. We, who can do things no other human can, and all we paid for the privilege was everything we had and ever were.

To Melory, I am just Handry, her brother.

And what is Melory to me? Sister, yes. Doctor, ghost-bearer. But more than that. Since unthroning Sharskin, she has become something else. She is the sage who interprets the voices that throng the House. She commands the ancestors and curates the fragmentary knowledge they deliver. She is the bridge between the villages and the Order, because although she commands the ancestors who shelter and feed us, she is not one of us.

She is the one who never abandoned me.

As we made our final approach to Meravo, we started the music. A few of us had pipes to blow into, tuneless but piercing. I have lived with the music for years, and it still scrapes about the inside of my head. Some had rattles of stones and gourds and bones. The rest had bells, just tubes hung from a string that we struck with stones. The tubes were metal, though, and metal was something the people of Meravo had no experience of, not a part of their world. The high, ringing tones of our bells, echoing out between the trees, told them something unnatural was drawing near. The Bandage-Men were coming to take their due.

And they would be rushing about, making their own preparations. There was a compact, between the Order and those villages that accepted us. Which were more than the villages that didn't, these days. It had been a long road: ten years, and I'm not the child I was when Sharskin found me starving in Orovo. And the villages would not have accepted that child, nor the man he grew into. But they would accept the Bandage-Men.

Back then, after I became the priest and Melory the sage; back then, when those of the Order who had not fled accepted the way things were . . . Back then we tried, Melory and I, to just go to the villages. To explain to them how it was, and that outcasts like me and the others were just people. And Melory was a ghost-bearer, an *expert system* as the ancestors named her. We thought they'd listen to her. But they looked on me, and they could not bridge that gap, even with Melory explaining.

They were bound in the web of the villages that tied everything together: the people, the ghosts, the tree with its hive, the wasps, even the vermin that lived on their bodies and fed on their blood. It was a system devised by the ancestors so that their descendants could live. The Severance removed its victims from that system. It removed from us the changes the ancestors had designed, that let people eat the fruit and meat of the world, handle its materials, yes, and catch its diseases and be devoured by its beasts, for that blade has two edges. More than that, it let them look on each other and know *That is one of us; that is human.* And, never having known a human not part of that system, they looked on me and saw a thing to fear. For, unbound by their unspoken rules and codes, I might do anything.

Yet we did find a way. We went to Orovo, where we knew Iblis, their Architect, was a woman who thought unusual thoughts. Melory spoke to ghost-bearers of many villages. She spoke to the ancestors and learned words and phrases that would let her conjure the ghosts and request their aid in brokering arrangements. Sometimes it worked; sometimes the ghosts refused to recognise her, and she talked distractedly of *versioning issues* and *failed backwards compatibility,* the jumble of sounds the ancients lapse into, as you approach the heart of their mystery. Some villages still refused to have us near and drove us off with sticks and slings. But not so many; not these days.

We became the wood-wanderers, the Bandage-Men, hedged about with our rituals. And in that way, with that careful measure of distance, the villages were able to come to terms with us. We had been Severed outcasts, thieves and murderers to be driven into the wilderness. Now the wilderness was our place and they knew we wouldn't just die, and so we came with our music and our wrappings. We came and made our camp outside the bounds of Meravo. We set our fire in their sight, not by arduous whirling of sticks, but with magic, which is to say a device of the ancestors we'd restored. We made our circle there, and we waited.

Over in the village, they'd taken some bread from that morning's baking and thrown it back in the oven, crisping it until half-black. Except I still remember the handful of years between my Severance and when I finally fled my home, and that burnt bread was all I could eat. So that had become part of the compact we made.

A little later, some child, perhaps bolder than the rest, came out carrying a basket of blackened loaves. He got as close as he dared, then dumped it in our sight and fled, squealing with his own daring. We made a great show of biting into the bread, though we had food brought from the House of our Ancestors that was far more palatable.

The village needed to see us accepting their offering, so they knew the compact still stood.

Then we rose, and there was more music, if that word can encompass the clatter and shriek we set riding on the breeze down into Meravo. Everyone was waiting for us there. The ghost-bearers of the village were before the tree, waiting for us. Everyone was nervous, a little frightened. Everyone was excited. And, if they'd been having problems, perhaps they were even relieved.

Meravo had a lawgiver and a doctor. They looked like ghost-bearers always do, like Melory does: their heads misshapen, lopsided, stippled with pits and holes. The Lawgiver was an old man with one eye completely eaten away where the ghost went in. The doctor was younger, my age, his forehead so swollen it gave him a permanent frown. I saw the ghostlight glimmer briefly in the sockets and apertures of both their faces as I approached.

We went about wrapped so that no inch of us showed, because the things of this world raise rashes and weals on our skin half the time, but many of us built on that appearance to grow our legend. There was a definite rhythm to our music, and some of my fellows danced to it, clapping, turning about, bowing and spinning. Many had bones and trophies strung about necks and wrists, or a whole vest of arraclid pieces woven together like armour. A couple had masks, horned, spiked, wild-eyed.

Just show, just nonsense, but even if the villagers didn't think of us as supernatural creatures, they knew we'd all done bad things, to become what we are. We got ourselves Severed, we were bad people, but the Order of Cain existed to make use of bad people.

At the back, Ledan bore the standard, something of an advertisement of the services we performed. The lattice-work skull of an arraclid recalled the first thing a Severed ever did for the villages, back when Iblis was expanding Orovo. *We hunt monsters.*

When we got to the heart of Meravo, I saw they had need of another service, as well. There was a young woman, standing off to one side of the ghost-bearers. Her head was down, and I saw bruises on her face and arms, most likely because she was the one villager who *didn't* want to be here.

At my signal, my fellows stopped, and I approached alone. I don't wear bone trophies or a mask, but I had the Eyes of the ancients, another device we restored at the House. Goggles, Melory calls them. I've had the ancestors show me what I look like with them on. Otherworldly, inhuman. A stare that passes through the merely physical and into the soul. I had Sharskin's staff, too, a metal shaft almost as tall as I was, my rod of office as priest.

Meravo's Lawgiver greeted me, that familiar battle behind his words: repulsion and fear and a grudging re-spect. We were things of the otherworld and, in being the one to speak to us, he bound us to the compact and re-minded everyone who was in charge. I asked if they had beasts that their hunters wished us to drive away from home or herd. He told me, no. The bruised woman was right there, but still I asked if there were any in Meravo who had the Lawgiver's judgment laid upon them. My followers made a show of staring about the crowd, espe-cially at the children. I heard a murmur go through them; people who were scared, but in a safe way. They knew that nobody was going to suddenly thrust them forth from the press to stand before us. Knowing that, they were free to imagine how it would be if it *did* happen.

But, no, the woman was being presented to us. Her name was Illon.

"Let her be brought to our camp beyond the village," I said, loud so all there could hear. "We must catechise her."

None of them knew what that meant. It was a word Melory learned from the ancestors. But it served, and the villagers expected the ritual. Illon was given into our care and two of my followers came, shaking their bone rattles so that she flinched, drawing her away by her wrists. And I could do this just sat in the doctor's hut or any secluded corner, but everyone there understood the significance of our taking Illon *out,* beyond the circle of their houses. Illon was trying to keep her head up, to put on a bold show for those who rejected her, but I saw how much she feared us. And she was right to.

In the old days, she'd have been Severed already. There would have been a different sort of festival, and people would have thronged to see her painted with the red mixture, turned into an unperson and driven out with stones and jeers. To die, most likely. Only a very few of us had lived, and mostly because the Lawgiver was slack in putting the Severance on, so it didn't quite take.

When we had her at our camp, the Order made a loose circle about her and me and the fire. I asked her, "What did you do?"

"Nothing," she said, sullen, and I repeated, "What did you *do*?" I've a special emphasis that told her this was the big question, one you don't lie to. I lifted the Eyes of the Ancients and she flinched, because my face didn't look like a living human face to her. Eyes, mouth, nose, beard, and yet there was no connection. Cast out, Severed, not part of her world.

A few of us got the Severance by accident, blameless and yet no less cut off from all we'd known. But most of us were villains of one stripe or another. Idlers, brawlers, thieves, troublemakers, murderers. Not the inhuman fiends the villagers like to think, but bad people. The Order exists to give a second chance to bad people.

"I knew better," she said. It started as a mumble, ended up a fierce growl. "I argued. Didn't do what the Lawgiver said. What the ghost said. Three times."

I watched her. I'd done this many times; the fear was my ally. Hard to tell a smooth lie when you're trembling before the Bandage-Men. I watched her and I waited as the cracks in her story spread.

"I hurt a woman," she said at last, baring her teeth. "She . . . I was jealous."

I waited.

"They told you this already," she hissed at last.

"They didn't. They will do, if I ask. But if you don't tell me, then there is no more between us."

Illon closed her eyes. "I was jealous, and so I waited for her, after dark. I waited until she came, and I beat her. I clubbed her down and hit her seven times."

Premeditated violence was a rare thing among the villagers. I saw in Illon someone whose whole life never quite fit the world she was born to. Someone destined to dance in the woods with the Bandage-Men.

"They told you that they'll give you to us," I said, and she nodded shortly. "Well that's not how it works."

Her turn to watch.

"We take none who don't come willingly. We are the Order of Cain. We bear the knowledge of the ancestors. We are outcasts, but we give to those who cast us out. Because we serve a greater purpose. We do work that none of the villagers understand. Walk with us and you must do as we do, perform what work is given you, obey when you are ordered. Or we will cast you out as well, and then there will be nowhere in this world that can shelter you, not the villages, not the forest, not the House of our Ancestors."

"And if I say no?" A lot of them don't even ask that, but I appreciate those who do.

"Then you are Severed and make your own way, and nobody will order you, and you will do no work you do not wish, and you will have no purpose, and all the world will be turned against you. But still I say, we take none who do not come willingly, and I will know if you merely feign when I demand the oaths from you."

That bit wasn't true, not really. I've been wrong before, though I am a good judge, I think. But it sounded impressive and most of our potential recruits believed it.

"It doesn't sound better than the village."

My smile must have looked terrible, the way she flinched from it. "But the village is not among your options, Illon. Your actions closed that door. And no, it is not better. I can't even swear it's better than dying alone in the woods. But it is something, and you will have comrades to share your misery."

We watched the doctor brew up the Severance and the

Lawgiver apply it. Not haphazardly or to his tastes, but with the sigils I showed him. The light touch would blunt the Severance a little, so that she might eat a berry or a sliver of meat from this world without it striking her dead of poison. The symbols spelled out her crime, but only I and two others there even read the ancestors' signs. The people of Meravo were solemn, reverent even. When we had gone, they'd have their feast and congratulate themselves on a job well done. And they would tell their stories of wicked Illon being tormented by the Bandage-Men, her feet whipped, driven howling through the trees. Or whatever the local variant of the story was.

The Lawgiver had some word to pass to nearby villages, and that was another of our services, for the village folk did not travel. The beasts of the wild were a terror to them; even their hunters never ventured far. Before we came, contact between the villages was a matter of once every few years. We had become a tenuous web of communication, carrying ideas, invitations, manifests of trade. I could almost feel the world becoming larger, for all these people, simply because we were in it.

At the end of all of this, we made our formal farewells. Illon came to us, and we wrapped her as one of our own. She was looking back for faces she knew, but none of them knew her anymore. She had passed into the shadow life that is our lot.

It was part of the ritual that I ask the Lawgiver, "Have the ancestors any word for their servants?" and I did not expect a reply. Yet the old man's head snapped back, and the ghostlight flared bright in all the blemishes and holes of his face.

"*System recognises Handry,*" came his cracked voice, the ghost speaking through him. "*Message follows: Make all haste to Orovo, brother. Message ends.*"

A chill went through me, even though this wasn't the first time; even though I knew the trick was no magic. The ghosts can speak across great distances. Even the little fragment of ghost Melory placed in me when we first parted could talk to her all the way over in Aro, telling her how I sickened and was hurt, letting her track me across the world. And so Melory found how to make the ancestors, who are just another kind of ghost, speak to the trees of all the villages. So she passed messages to the wanderers of the Order who otherwise would be cut off from all news until they returned home.

But I had not looked for news, still less a summons. We lived in a slow world where each day and each season was little different. Melory would not call me unless something unprecedented had happened.

We left first thing the next morning, and it seemed Illon would get a swift and unorthodox introduction to the secrets of our Order.

II

THE HOUSE OF OUR Ancestors sailed the night sky from another world. Those it brought here were hero-people, masters of making and doing and knowing. And yet this land proved their equal, and they made their own compact with it, just as the villages make their compact with us. They gave up the Original Condition of mankind, which is to be cold and hungry and despised. And, because they loved their children, they gave them ghosts to guide them, the expert systems who always knew best. I remember Sharskin telling me. He said the world had not changed for five hundred years, while the House of our Ancestors fell into ruin.

The House of our Ancestors is the heart of our world, a secret we do not speak of to the villages, even though it is the heart of their world, too. The heart, because the ancestors are everyone's ancestors. The heart, because Melory drew a map, once, and the villages formed an expanding ring about a hollow, unsettled centre, and in that centre lay the House, surrounded by a ruin of failed communities from when the ancestors were still trying to reach their compact with the world.

The other landmark for us in our wanderings is Orovo.

Orovo was where it all started. That was where I met Sharskin the priest, and where Iblis the Architect first looked on the Severed and saw something she could use. I met Sharskin in Orovo because they had food there for outcasts who would hunt beasts for them, clearing the land around a new tree so that half Orovo's overburdened people could find a second home. And I have watched that new village, Orovillo as they call it; watched it grow and prosper, and felt a curious pride, for my little part in bringing it about. But Iblis paved the way for the Order before the Order was anything other than Sharskin's cult, and it was her path Melory and I followed later, when Sharskin was dead.

We passed through the forests at the best pace Illon could make. She was terrified at first; everyone is. The beasts of the woods would devour a hapless villager caught alone amidst the trees. On the third day, I found the track of a mereclet, where its two-clawed prongs had scarred the trunks. We followed it until we came to its den and it waddled out to inspect us: a fat-bodied, spike-armoured thing on six barbed legs with a fist of sawing arms that could turn man to meat in the blink of an eye. It threatened us, and if we'd bothered it too much, it might attack simply to drive us away, but it showed no appetite for our flesh.

"We cannot eat of the flesh of beasts, nor fruit, nor any thing of the world," I told Illon. "Nor can they eat of us. We are Severed from all of it." And I gave her the ancestors' food, the soft, sweet, wrapped sticks from the House, and we left the mereclet alone.

I wondered if it was as simple as that: that Orovo had an animal problem again that needed sorting. Orovo was the largest of all the villages I had seen, and the Bandage-Men brought their dolorous music there often. They didn't like us—they *couldn't* like us—but they remembered. I think Iblis liked us a bit, because her mind worked differently, and because she was used to arguing with the ghost.

As it turned out, it was something very different.

We came to Orovo with our rattles and bells, striding along the new hard-packed paths they had there, another Iblis idea. People stopped to stare, and we picked up a tail of children playing at how close they could come to our heels before we looked back at them. Familiarity takes the edge off the strangeness. Orovo was a safe haven for any of the Order seeking shelter.

They didn't have a grand welcome for us there, not when some wanderer band came in and out every twenty days, and not with Orovo such a grand place, its ghost-bearers constantly overworked. What we did get was Iblis and Melory hurrying to intercept us before we got near the tree.

Melory and I embraced. I pulled away my goggles and made myself look into her face, and she made herself look into mine. Her difficulty was my Severance, for she was still *village* despite all her ties to the Order. My difficulty was what the ghost made of her, when it made its home in her skull. A face not unlike my own, once, but now pushed out, swollen in parts, fallen in elsewhere, and one eye closed up and destroyed. Never easy, but I always made myself do it: say *Sister* even as she reminds herself, *Brother.*

Iblis was a tall woman, greying now, who looked like she was half smiling, one corner of her mouth trapped upwards by the deformations the ghost gave her. Her real smiles weren't much more than that, and she just nodded distractedly at me. Iblis tended to have two roads into any conversation: to say nothing or to say all of it. The only time I ever heard real give and take with her was when she was talking to her ghost, its words and her words going back and forth out of her mouth, all in her voice. It wasn't something Melory did with her own doctor ghost, nor any other bearer. But, like I say, Iblis was always different.

Orovo kept a building in sight of its tree that no local lives in. We called it the Little House and it was for us, one more concession Iblis talked her ghost into. In the Little House we put down our packs and I deputised Ledan to get people mending and cleaning and setting the fire, and to make sure Illon did a share of the work.

"Now." I sat with Melory and Iblis. "What's gone on?"

"We've had a visitor," Melory told me. "A new expert system."

I didn't know what to make of that. Villagers seldom travel, but when they do, it's never the ghost-bearers themselves. Far too precious. And then I considered what she'd just said. "Not just a new bearer?"

"A new type of expert system. Not even an old one that fell out of use, but something completely new."

I looked from her to Iblis, who shrugged. Iblis had visited the House of our Ancestors once, much to the horror of Orovo's people. She'd spoken to the ghostly voices that lived in those metal halls and shared something of Melory's communion with them. Still, Melory had been ten years at study and still only understood a little. Iblis could have spent all her days learning merely that the abyss was wider than anyone suspected.

But new expert systems was a topic Melory was deeply invested in, for the Order's sake. Melory thought it possible to breed a new ghost, an ambassador who could be of the villages and yet of *us* as well.

But this new visitor hadn't got Melory excited, only worried.

"How do you know it's completely new?" There were many ghosts almost nobody met, arising in response to some rare resource or danger.

"It's here because of you, the Order. The bearer says she's a Champion, but I think the ancestors would have called her an antibody. Something that arises in response to a disease, to defend against it. She's here from Jalaino."

One of the villages that had never accepted us. "How can they make a new ghost?"

"When hives are grown for new villages, they aren't perfect copies," Melory said slowly. "Iblis says she can already see that Orovillo's hive is a little different from Orovo that birthed it. And over time, I think, each hive gets more different. It makes its own decisions, makes new laws, gathers new knowledge . . . When I came to the House of our Ancestors, Handry, you remember how it was. The ghost in me, the ancestors in the House, they couldn't talk to each other straight away. They had to change themselves to find that middle ground."

She said it so calmly, but it had been a traumatic thing. Of course, Sharskin was priest then, and a lot of the trauma had come from him.

"The Jalaino hive is . . . difficult. They haven't responded to our overtures at all, but I think the fact of the

Order set something in motion, caused a reaction there. The hive sees you as a threat, and this new ghost is their response."

She must have heard that the Bandage-Men had come to Orovo because she was waiting for us beneath the eaves of the Lawgiver's house, next to the tree. What struck me first was her size, taller than me and far broader about the shoulders beneath her cloak. Melory's briefing explained what lay underneath: not ghost-twisted musculature, or not just that. She had come armoured; more, she had come alone. I say that villagers don't travel and yet here was someone who'd walked to Orovo from Jalaino, a trek of many days.

I called. "I am Handry of the Order of Cain." I had a dozen of the Order at my back, people like Ledan, hardened to the wandering life. I walked to within ten feet of her, gazed on her through the Eyes of the Ancestors, planted my metal staff in the earth. On all sides, from between houses and out of windows, the people of Orovo tried to pretend they weren't watching.

She stiffened. A twitch of her head cast back her cowl and she shrugged away her cloak, freeing herself in case it was to be a fight then and there. I saw a woman's face, thin and lean and still with both her eyes. Her cheeks were hollow like a starveling's. The hair she had left was pale and lank and only on one side of her head. The other side was stippled with dents, pushed out over her ear. The ghostlight burned there like the final embers of last night's fire. About her shoulders, forming the hunch of her back, she wore a great knotted mass of wood, familiar in its contours and structure from the hive at every village's heart. Insects crawled in and out of its galls and sockets, finger-length wasps of iridescent blue and green that flexed their wings in a murmurous buzz; that took to the air and described a looping cordon around her.

"I am Amorket of Jalaino." Her voice sounded savage and hateful, but I had the benefit of Melory to advise me, and I knew what lay behind it. Even so prepared, I had to plant my will like I did my staff, to stand my ground there. The wasps glittered and spun in the sunlight, and *they* hated me. They were hatched for no other purpose but to destroy things like me. If Amorket had met me on the road before coming to Orovo, I had no doubt she would have killed me first, and only then asked if it would have helped anything.

But it was Melory she met, when she came here hunting the Order. Melory, who was of her world, a villager, a ghost-bearer. Melory, who was a doctor and knew pain when she saw it.

She'd told me how it had gone, between them. The madwoman in her living armour who came to Orovo's Lawgiver, demanding that the Severed be delivered up to her. Pounding on doors, screeching in at windows, the air about her busy with murderous insects. Only Melory and Iblis had dared approach her, the one for worry, the other out of curiosity.

At first all they'd got from Amorket was that she had been sent from Jalaino to purge the world of us. But Melory had seen the taut waxiness of the woman's face, the weariness, the pain-lines about her eyes. Melory reached out and touched her, and the doctor ghost spoke a long list of ailments and possible cures. So it was that the first armour of Amorket was breached.

"My sister has told me of you, and your mission," I said, fighting to keep my voice steady. There was a tone to those wasps that spoke fear into my mind, and it was hard to simply stand there. "Iblis the Architect has offered her house, for us to talk in private." To the great disappointment of every eavesdropper in Orovo, no doubt.

"I'm here to fight you." The words spat out fiercely but the eyes uncertain, almost pleading.

"If that is how it ends, then so be it," I said, as I agreed with Melory. "But we do not know how it ends. Come. My sister will ease your body, and we can talk."

~

Inside, at Melory's request, she doffed the armour that

served as a house for her Furies, as she called the wasps she carried. The gaunt, misshapen body beneath told me the insects were not hatched from the knots of her mail but grew from her own flesh. Amorket's back, breasts and belly were riddled with scars where the latest brood had gnawed its way free, and Melory said there were newer eggs still within her. She was a walking hive; Iblis said she must be a corruption of the process used to seed a new village. For her part, the Architect found Amorket infinitely fascinating.

"We go where we are invited," I said. "Jalaino does not want us. We do not go there."

"You change everything," Amorket grated through clenched teeth. "I have seen it. Every village between home and here is different. They welcome you in. They are no longer like my home."

"You never saw them before, to know if they were ever like your home," Iblis observed, more a point of logic than an attempt to persuade.

"You are a threat, or else why am I? Why are any of us?"

When Melory first spoke to her, Amorket maintained her home had sent her hunting us. But that was her word, not Jalaino's. Sympathy and medicine and careful questions had teased out the truth, at once stranger and worse.

"Melory says there are many of you now, in your

home. Many . . . Champions?"

The fire flickered in her face and, simultaneously, in all the pocks and burrows of her body, and she flinched with it. "Many," she agreed, staring at me with disgust, but with something else, too. I think it might be hope.

The Jalaino hive had gone mad in its fear of us. There were a dozen Champions there, and Jalaino was not large. More Champions than all the other ghosts combined, and the Elector wasps still issuing from the hive. It was, Melory said, like an allergic reaction. Like the very thing that raised rashes on my bare hands when I touched some plant or beast's hide. It was defence overgrown until it strangled what it sought to preserve.

"You came here yourself," I said quietly. "To kill us all, without knowing how many we are or even what we are."

"A danger," she said, words coming by rote. Melory gave her a steaming cup of something cooked up on Iblis's fire and she drank eagerly.

"I want to bring her to the House," Melory put in, but I shot her a warning glance. If this business with Jalaino went badly, I didn't want them knowing where the ancestors lived.

"If you understood," I told her, calm even though there were wasps crawling about Iblis's ceiling, "then you might see we are not a threat, but a blessing: we drive off beasts, we take away your Severed, we—"

"Change," she hissed, but then she drank, and some of the tension went out of her as the medicine went in. I heard a quiet sob she couldn't bottle up. A new ghost, a new expert system as Melory said; one not comfortable in its human skin.

"And yet we talk," I noted, pushing my luck.

She stared bleakly at me, but in that look, I could read a plea. *Help us find a way out.* From what she told Melory, Jalaino could barely support all its newfound ghost-bearers, men and women tortured by what they had become, blundering about the village like wasps themselves. One went mad, she said, killed two people and had to be killed in turn, the pain too much, the twisting of their body, the constant voices of the wasps.

Then someone outside called my name, and the wasps were abruptly all in the air, spiralling about the confines of Iblis's house, in constant danger of falling into the fire. I rose slowly, carefully, eyes on Amorket.

"What is it? Is that Graf I hear?" He led another band of ours that should have been days out of Orovo.

"Priest," came the call from outside. "We're come from Tsuno to get word to you. Hardly let our heels cool since we left it." A village on his route, towards the edge of where people lived. A frontier place, nowhere anything important happened, surely, and yet here was Graf telling me, "They need help, priest. They have a war."

III

THE ANCESTORS SAY THAT war was once a thing people did to each other. Whole villages would go and fight other villages. When I heard that, I couldn't imagine it. I couldn't imagine why. Now, having met Amorket, I have a bad feeling that such things could happen after all. Jalaino has gone wrong; it fears and, in its fear, its hive is building a pressure that must be bled off. Or else explode.

But war, to us, is not people against people. It is when people fight animals, but not hunting. War was what Orovo was recruiting outcasts for, all those years ago. They needed to clear a new tree of beasts, and there was a village of harboons there that wouldn't move. Not a real village, of course, but they had their little houses in the branches, and probably the harboons thought of it as their village. And then we outcasts came, who didn't get poisoned by their darts, and who were unnatural and strange, and we broke their houses and drove them away. And that was the end of the war, and Iblis could claim the new tree, and now that's where Orovillo stands.

In the Little House, Graf told me all he knew. He

hadn't got to Tsuno himself. Tsuno had actually sent people to the nearest villages looking for the Order. What they'd told Graf was that they didn't want to go make war on some animals. Instead, some animals had come to make war on them.

Graf was a big man, Severed for killing someone in an argument. A bad man, but he took to the Order and the travelling life. "Brackers," he told me. Nothing I'd seen or met, but he'd seen some, once. "Big things, twice the size of us. Their places are past Tsuno and Farro, off beyond where people live. Or they were. And if you ask me, people don't live there because the brackers do."

We made arrangements then: Ledan to take three or four and continue on our route, visiting the villages and doing what needed to be done. I and the rest of our band to go with Graf and his people and see what was happening at Tsuno.

Which left Jalaino as a thorn in my mind I couldn't pluck out, and my heart told me it'd be a bigger problem than any number of animals.

However, when I explained all this to Melory, I found my problems weren't going to separate themselves out so neatly after all.

"Amorket says she'll travel with you."

The Champion of Jalaino sat outside the Lawgiver's house, cloak over her bulky armour. With one knee drawn up to her sharp chin, she looked almost childlike.

"She thinks it will help her work out what to do," Melory told me.

"And if she decides she has to kill me?"

"Then you'll be surrounded by your own people, at least. And you're going to help a village. If she goes back to Jalaino and tells them . . ." But her words petered out.

"You don't believe that," I decided.

"I don't think it can work like that, no," she agreed reluctantly. "Because we're not just dealing with some villagers who don't like you. We're dealing with a hive that has set itself against you. It's producing these Champions to fight you. If I could go there, then perhaps I could open a channel to it, but . . ."

"But it might kill you. She said one of the other Champions already ran mad." Right then, all the pressures of being priest of the Order seemed too much. It's hard at the best of times, with the world poison and all the rest looking to you. And now a village wanted to destroy us, and who knew how that idea might spread.

"Let her come with us. Either that or she follows us anyway, and better we have her where we can see her."

"And I'll be there," Melory put in. I eyed her, but of course she'd come. She'd been looking out for me since before I was Severed; she wouldn't stop now.

~

The next morning, Iblis saw us off with her crooked smile. She cast a wry glance at Amorket, standing apart from us like a shadow.

"Probably there'll be three more like her waiting, when you come back." Said mostly to see how I'd react. The prospect seemed all too likely. From what Amorket said, the hive at Jalaino wouldn't stop until it felt safe from us.

I hoped Amorket wouldn't be able to keep up with us. I've seen strong-seeming new recruits falter, after a few days in the wilds. Villagers work hard at their farms and crafts, but travelling needs a different kind of strength.

And yet, when we set camp the first dusk, Amorket was still with us. She walked our trail all the way, ten, twenty feet behind us, never out of sight. Perhaps she told herself she was hunting us, and thus appeased the ghost within her. She didn't share our fire, but made her own within our view. In the morning, she was awake and ready to go by the time we rose. No predator appeared to rid us of her, and reaching Orovo without an escort showed she was more than capable of defending herself.

"She doesn't eat." Graf had barely taken his eyes off her since she joined us.

"I think the wasps eat," was Melory's best guess. "And

then they go back into their house, and they feed her even as they feed on her. She doesn't get tired, because they won't let her."

"Lucky her," Graf decided, but Melory shook her head at that.

"No, because you need to get tired. It's your body's way of telling you to rest. Only she doesn't have that. She's burning herself up, just being who she is."

Good, I thought, but Melory felt sorry for this Amorket; this Champion who'd sworn to destroy me. Melory was the doctor ghost's bearer, after all. She couldn't help wanting to make people whole.

So it went all the way to Tsuno: long days of tramping between the trees following the paths we of the Order worked out. Landmark to landmark, rivers and rises. Here and there a marker left by past travellers: distances and directions carved into stones in the simple code we taught each other, boiled down from the sigils the ancestors used to preserve their knowledge. Because the call was urgent, we pushed harder than normal, and at night there was less talk because everyone was tired. And always Amorket followed like a worry that would not go away. Until I realised she was becoming for me what I was to the villages: a personification of what there was in the world to fear. She is what I would warn my children about.

That made me think of Illon, because she was as close to a child as any of the Order would ever have. I had not sent her away with Ledan; there was a rebellious streak in her, not unusual for the newly Severed. She was cast out because she would not live within the rules of a village. She must learn to live within the rules of the Order, or she would be cast out twice over. So I took her to war instead.

Here was a secret I would not tell Amorket, because it would be giving a knife to my enemy. We had no children. Sharskin's iron rule that no man of his followers lie with a woman remained in force. The child sickened, the mother sickened. Both died as the world rejected them. Melory was working with all the lore of the ancestors to overcome it, but until she succeeded, people like Illon were the only new blood the Order ever saw.

~

And then we came to Tsuno.

There were too many people crammed into a small village. People and ertibeests and shrovers and a host of little two-legged beasts Graf called moxies. And there was a wall, about two-thirds built. The architect ghost of Tsuno had found a pattern for something previously unnecessary.

We came out past the stumps of all the trees that got cut for that wall. It was going on for dusk, but we could see people still digging footings and driving logs in, lashing each to its neighbour. Brackers were big, Graf said, and the wall was made of massive trunks, set next to one another so you could barely get a knifeblade in between them. The sight made me nervous, and I understood a little about Amorket and Jalaino, seeing change in the world and not liking it at all.

Still, they were pleased to see us. Not just the stand-offish pleased we get when we turn up with our wild music and our bandages. Word spread so that all of Tsuno was looking at us when we stepped over the most recent postholes and into the village.

Tsuno was small, but with everyone pulled in from the fields and the herds, with all their animals jostling and complaining and stinking, it felt big and crowded, almost like Orovo did back before they split. All those people looked at us with an expression I'm not used to: desperate hope. We outcasts were what they'd fixed on, to save them from these brackers.

And they stared at Amorket, stalking in our footsteps. They could see she wasn't one of us, but she wasn't one of them, either. The thought hit me with a stab of sympathy I didn't really want. As a professional outsider, I couldn't help being sorry for someone who had even less a place in the world than me.

Soon after that, with only the briefest nod at all the ritual greeting we were used to, Graf and Melory and I were hustled up before Tsuno's Lawgiver.

~

He looked like he wasn't older than fourteen years, and that couldn't be helping matters. At first, I assumed this was bad luck; that their last Lawgiver just died of being old at precisely the wrong time. But no, as the story came out. Their last Lawgiver went to drive away the brackers, and the brackers did for him. The child I saw before me had been Lawgiver for no more than twenty days, and he was terrified. The ghost had to fight to speak through him. And the ghost wasn't much help because this hadn't happened before, and there was no law for the Lawgiver to give. The one thing they knew was that, if you have an animal problem, you ask the Order.

This wouldn't be like driving arraclids from the herds, though. From what they were saying, it wouldn't even be like driving harboons out for Orovo.

"We first saw them a hundred days ago," the Lawgiver told us. His voice trembled so much I felt he was still at his mother's teat a hundred days ago. "Brackers live north and east, always. We don't go to their lands, they don't come to ours. That's how it always was, before. A hundred days ago, hunters started to see bracker trails in our hunting grounds." And I understood his *hundred days* didn't mean that. I was too used to the ancestors who were precise in everything they measure. His *hundred days* meant long ago but not that long.

"Then we started to find their houses, where they'd built. They brought their herds to where our herds were. They stole from our fields before the harvest was ready. We tried to drive them off, but then there were more of them than anyone had ever seen, and they just took what they wanted. Then the Lawgiver killed one. Then more came and killed him. In sight of the village."

"They eat your flesh?" Graf asked right out.

The Lawgiver paled. "They eat no flesh, not even their herd beasts. But they are not shy of killing. I'll send for our best hunter. She has seen more than I have." And that I didn't doubt, because I suspected this boy had seen next to nothing.

"Bring her in, if she'll sit with us," I invited. His eyes flicked between us, over and over to Melory because he couldn't work out where she fitted. I was too tired with the story to tell him.

The hunter was a hard woman, older than anyone else there, her short hair grey but her body still strong. Erma, the Lawgiver called her, and she looked me and Graf up and down. She looked me right in the Eyes of the Ancestors and didn't flinch. She'd seen worse than me, that look said.

"I know brackers," she said. "This isn't what they do, never before. Keep to their own places."

"You went hunting them with the other Lawgiver?" Melory asked her.

"No. I told them not to." Erma scowled. "Leave it to the hunters. But the Lawgiver wouldn't have it." And it's not often you find a villager who'll argue with a lawgiver. This old woman might have been one of us, if she'd gone only a little off her path. And the boy glowered at her for questioning his predecessor, even after what happened.

"What has the Lawgiver said?" The way I said it made clear what I meant.

The boy wouldn't look at me. "The hunters and herders are to train more of their trades, more spears and slings. Everyone who can. So we can fight."

It was a reasonable response from the ghost: gather in more of the most needed resource, in this case hands that could defend the village. Perhaps that and the wall would be enough. Without seeing the brackers, I couldn't know.

"Erma," I said. "Can you tell me of the land the brackers have seized?"

She nodded, watching me carefully. She was of the villages and I was of the Order, but right then there was a bridge across that gap; she and I understood one another.

"Lawgiver, we will scout tomorrow. May Erma come to our fire tonight, and tell us what we need to know?" Specifically, tell us whatever might not get said in the Lawgiver's earshot.

~

We camped hard up against the wall, close to the ragged edge where they were still building. There was no room for us inside, everyone so crammed in and frightened that having the Severed at their elbow would be inviting trouble. Erma's visit was brief. She could be as hardy as she liked, but sitting with us made her profoundly edgy.

"I know these brackers," she told us. "I know them all—there's five, six villages of them over in their lands. They paint themselves, coloured mud and stuff squeezed from plants. Looks a bit like this, even." She flicked a finger at the red stain down one side of my face, where I'd loosened my bandages. "So this village used to live days away, other side of Portruno. That's a place right on the edge of the wilds, you know it?"

None of us had been there. The Order had come to Tsuno twice in ten years, but no further.

"I tried to make the Lawgiver see, but he says other villages aren't our business," Erma told us. "But to come here, they came through Portruno. I want to go see what happened there."

The Lawgiver wouldn't let her. But the Lawgiver *would* let her guide us, and didn't decide where we went.

IV

FROM TSUNO WE COULD look northeast and see the mountains that were the northern edge of where people lived. Westwards, the land fell away down densely wooden slopes of red and orange-leaved trees. That was where the brackers were supposed to stay with their herds and their houses. People had never tried to contest them for it because the soil was poor and the stinging rains frequent, so that even the trees crept slowly about on their roots and jostled for the best places.

Erma took us that way: Melory and me, Kalloi and Il-lon of my people, and the unwelcome shadow that was Amorket. I left Graf with most of my Bandage-Men back at Tsuno to scare off the brackers if they came. We kept well clear of the brackers' new village, and I wondered if the beasts had a problem like Orovo, too many of them in one place, so they needed to spread elsewhere. Were the people of Tsuno to them like the harboons had been to Iblis, just something to be chased off so they could live there? Was Portruno already a bracker village?

When we reached Portruno, though, the brackers

weren't living there. Nothing was.

Nothing was standing. Every house had been torn down. With some, it seemed the staves of the walls had been pulled methodically outwards. Others had been pushed in, flattened as though boulders had been rolled over them.

The tree, which was every village's heart, was on its side, trunk splintered, branches shattered, its roots clawing at the air.

The *tree*.

For a moment, I couldn't think. Erma, Melory, we all just stared. Somehow it was Amorket who brought me back to myself.

"I didn't think you would care," she said, and abruptly I realised the flecks at the corner of my vision were her wasps. I was within their angry circle; she was right at my shoulder. "You're not of *this* anymore. What is it to you?"

"It is still the world," I managed. "It hates us, but we are in it. The world is a certain way. The trees . . ." I had seen dead villages, failed villages, but they were old. The forest around the House of our Ancestors was littered with them, from before the ancestors perfected their plans. But never since then. People die, houses fall down, but the *village* lives forever. That's what it's for.

"I can't feel it." Amorket's tight, unwelcome voice, each word as though it were forced out of her by hand. "I *know*, but I can't. There's no room in me."

"Because you're full of hate for me and mine."

"Yes." A single, despairing curse of a word, because that hate wasn't even hers, but a thing she'd been forced to don with that armour and the wasps that went in and out of her flesh. And, like those wasps, it had eaten out a space to dwell in, and now there were parts of Amorket's mind that existed only to the extent that she recognised their absence. She was like those lost villages of the ancestors, a failed experiment.

But that didn't mean I had to be sympathetic, and it didn't mean she wouldn't kill me, by choice or because she had no choice.

"Bodies, priest," said Kalloi. It was no great feat of perception on his part. There were bodies everywhere, or mostly pieces of bodies. Not enough, I thought, for a whole village's worth, but many. The scavengers were already about them. Larger beasts had doubtless hauled off their meals elsewhere, but the busy little life of the world scattered only reluctantly at our tread, lifting into the air or burrowing into the earth. I saw hands, legs, ribs, the solid bones unique to the descendants of the ancestors.

And there was a trail, or at least a furrowing of the earth all around the wreck of Portruno. The fields were half torn up, the corrals, everything. I did my best to read it, but the sheer wealth of tracks defeated me. It was just a colossal disturbance of the ground that came, circled all round and through the village, and then left by the same route.

"Erma." My voice, raised to reach her ear, was far too loud in this dead space. I expected a ghastly, tormented look from her, but what I got was the face of a woman wrestling with deductions already. Tsuno had a good lead hunter.

"These brackers, Graf said they were big. How big, exactly?"

"Twice my size, full grown." Her eyes scattered over the devastation. "Yes, they could tear down a house, one or two of them."

"And the tree?"

It was too much of a question; nobody had ever considered what it might take, to bring such a giant to the earth. But then she said, "They never did anything like this before."

"You've lived with them on your border," Melory noted. "There must have been friction. Some man of Portruno killed one of theirs, maybe? Took something they held dear? Broke their eggs?"

"Don't have eggs," Erma corrected automatically, eyes still not quite able to stay still on anything. "I've known brackers since my Ma showed me where their places were. Never anything like this." She stalked through the ruin, going to see the trail out.

"Change," Amorket pronounced, and I turned on her in case she was about to make this about *us,* as though the Order's mere existence could have tilted some intrinsic balance in the world. From her expression, she was arguing with something inside rather than picking a fight with me.

"Erma." Melory picked her way after, grimacing. "You and your hunters keep an eye on them, these brackers?"

Erma's pretence at not hearing her was obvious even to me.

"You just mark their places and stay away, or you go back and see what they're doing? Big neighbours, and many. I'd want to know."

"You're asking if we saw this brewing?"

"I'm asking what you're not saying out loud."

The hunter stopped still, staring out into where the tree line started, at the edge of what had been Portruno's fields.

"What are you, ghost-bearer?" I could barely catch her voice. "You come here with the outcasts, but you're blessed of the tree. And *her,*" no need to even point Amorket out, "still less anything I understand. Will that ghost you carry call me out to the Lawgiver, do you think?"

I frowned at Melory, not sure where the words were leading.

"My ghost's a doctor, and I've fought it down before. I am . . ." And what, exactly, was Melory now? "A scholar. I dwell among the Bandage-Men. I know more than any living about the ghosts and our ancestors and all the secret things of the past." No idle boast. "So tell me."

"When I was little," Erma said, still facing away from us, "my Ma took me to where the brackers live, just as her Ma did with her, just as I've done with all three of mine that lived to an age for it. She took me to where a pole was stuck in the ground, a clear space no tree would move to. The ground was crusty with white crystals the brackers crap out. She had a wooden carving, held it in her two hands. I never could make out what it was of, but it was stained red as Severance. She set that on the pole, and she blew a pipe she had with her, that made no sound at all, and we sat down to wait. And the brackers came."

At last she turned back to us. "Three of them, bigger than I'd ever thought. So scared, I was. But my Ma, she went to them and started making marks in the ground, just slashes: she does three, then they do two. She does four, then they do three. Or maybe it was different numbers. Done it enough myself, since, that I don't rightly recall.

"They go then, and I'm asking and I'm asking when can we go home and what was all that? But we spend all night there, me twitching at every sound, sure the brackers are coming back to kill and eat us. And next morning, there they are. And they have a handful of game—just broken animal bodies, a mereclet, a couple of vissids. Things we wouldn't hunt but that I'd seen driven off from the fields before. And they have some of this . . . hair, fur. It's from their beasts, I know now. This cloth." She tugged at her tunic. "Lasts near forever, keeps out the wet. *Hunters' shirts* they call these, back home. Only we get to wear them, because only we know where the weave comes from. So they give us this, and Ma has her sack open and hands over some knives and some pots, even a gourd of tunny, and they match these things up one against the other, so I can see the same numbers there, as the scratches in the earth: some of *these* for some of *those.* You understand?"

"Your Ma *traded* with them?" asked Melory, wide-eyed.

"Not just her," as though it was an accusation. "All the hunters. All of us who become hunters get shown it. It's the way, but . . ."

"The Lawgiver can't know."

"It's not ghost business," Erma said sullenly. "Right from the start, the ghosts say, keep away from the brackers. They have their places and we have ours. Only . . ."

A tradition. What she had was what we have built these last ten years. A new way of doing things, a mystery, an Order. I couldn't imagine what hard times or chance meeting led to what she's describing, but I understood how it had been perpetuated, passed down one hunter to the next. Knowledge learned and taught, not simply distributed by a ghost. I could curse, that we only discovered this *now*, when the brackers had gone mad and destroyed a village, when this mystery of Erma's was of no use to anyone.

I wondered what Sharskin would have made of it. Even after all this time my thoughts still went to him. Would he have welcomed this sign that people had made something of their own, without the ghosts? Or would he have crushed it, because it was not his?

After that, we made to leave Portruno to the scavengers. Perhaps people would travel here to recover anything left unbroken. Crafted things were valuable, after all, though there was little that had not been . . .

I wanted to say *smashed*. I wanted to cast what I was seeing as mindless devastation: the beasts had run mad, as it is easy to imagine beasts doing. But the more I looked at the ruin, the more I saw fragments of pattern.

Melory had seen it, too. She was standing by a flattened house, looking at objects strewn next to where its entrance would have been. Except they were not strewn. The word was *arranged*. There was a hoe, a rake, a knife, an arm. The hand was attached, but the fingers had been pulled off and set beside the knife, longest first. The whole sequence was in order of length. It was not an animal thing to do. It had a dreadful sense of a child's game played with grisly pieces.

Seeing that, we saw odd elements everywhere we looked. A circle of disjointed limbs, arranged so that the large ends all met in the centre; a house where the curved staves of the walls had been stacked neatly one atop another; a clutch of tree branches snapped off that had been leant together as though to form a model of the uprooted original. There was something chilling in it all, past mere death and ruin.

I'd been a wanderer ten years. I had travelled from village to village, creating the traditions that kept the Order alive. The forest was my place. But now I looked into the trees and shivered.

At our call, Erma turned from the tracks and led us back towards Tsuno. In all our minds, no doubt, was the fear that we would find another ruin, another toppled tree, all my followers vanished or torn apart trying to defend the place. We were strong against beasts, we of the Order. Animals were as frightened of us as people. Except these brackers were not acting like animals, and so our greatest weapon might mean nothing.

We came back to Tsuno to find it still there; no bracker had come near it yet. However there was news. Some of Erma's hunters had gone to spy on the new village the brackers were building for themselves on Tsuno land. They reported that the brackers had a human prisoner amongst them. More, they said it was no villager; it was one of ours.

V

THERE WAS A LOT of talking late into the night, and it went nowhere. The Lawgiver, that frightened boy, he spoke, and his ghost spoke, and neither of them had anything useful to say. Amorket is living proof that villages and their ghosts are not good at reacting to new things.

Melory stood before the tree at Tsuno and sent word to the House of our Ancestors. The invisible voices there would remember what she had said and speak it back to Ostel and the others. There would be no help from so far away, though. And if the ghosts couldn't help, then likely the ancestors couldn't help, either.

I spoke to my people of what we saw at Portruno, and that the brackers might not be driven off like beasts are. As for the supposed prisoner, none of us was missing, and Graf didn't think any other band of the Order would be travelling near here. The brackers had some poor Severed outcast from Portruno, perhaps.

Erma came to our camp to say she would go to the bracker village. She would try the traditions of her mystery. "It's all we have," she said. There was no hunter ghost to guide her, but if there was, it would be in the same position as the rest. The brackers had lived as careful neighbours of the people here for as long as anyone knew; Erma's mystery was old when her Great-Grandma took her Grandma out into the woods, showed her the carving and blew the soundless whistle.

They wanted us to go and fight, in the morning. Because the ghosts had no words and they were all frightened, they wanted to hide behind their part-built wall and have us go and drive the brackers away. For our part, the Order had to do something. This was what we were for, the greatest service we gave to the villages. In return for this, they overlooked our nature, they let us have their unwanted and did not hunt us. Their hate for us became just the fear of children. *The Bandage-Men will get you.* They knew that if both sides respected the traditions, they would be safe. But part of those traditions was that, when people and animals cannot live together, the Bandage-Men fight for the people against the world.

I did not see this going well and so I talked to Erma about how she might use her mystery, and how we could help her. The whole night was one kind of talk or another. Of those who had come to the aid of Tsuno, only one wasn't talking.

In the morning, Amorket had already gone.

For just a moment I thought she might simply have

gone back towards Jalaino, or even wandered off into the woods to die. Melory knew better. Amorket was the doctor ghost's patient and, just as she could track me all those years ago, she knew exactly where Amorket was headed. Towards the new village the brackers were building. She had gone to fight for Tsuno, alone.

For me, I said let her go, but Melory and Erma both insisted we follow her. Erma feared Amorket would rile up the brackers even more and make the work of her mystery that much harder. Melory . . . At first I thought it was just the duty of the doctor to a patient, but on the way she told me, "Amorket is not the problem, Handry. Jalaino is the problem. Other villages might go the same way. That is what we need to solve. And Amorket is my only tool, to understand them."

～

Erma, Melory and I, with half my people, followed the clear set of tracks Amorket had left. We heard her before we saw her: a thin, high human voice raised in angry challenge. We didn't hear the bracker. When we burst from the trees and saw it, I felt very much like turning around and just going away again. I'd imagined something like a harboon, only bigger.

Like most animals, it had six legs. The first set were

largest, elbows higher than its body, feet like the knotted heads of clubs. I could imagine them smashing down a house very easily. Its hide was greyish and warty, thick and ridged about those front legs. Its back legs were short and stumpy; if nothing else, I reckoned I could outrun it easily enough. The middle legs were arms, slender and folded under its broad, flat body. I saw three thick pads on them like fat fingers.

Its head was small for its body. Four eyes jutted on thumb-like jointed stalks, one either side, two below. Unlike most animals it couldn't see straight up, and I was already thinking about treetop ambushes, dropped rocks. In front of the eyes there was a clutch of mouthparts like a webbed hand with six long fingers. Behind them were round discs of smooth skin, big ones and small ones.

It had been painted. There were designs on the armour of its forelegs, and on its back, where it couldn't even see. They were symmetrical, flowing, reminding me of the shape of certain plants, how they branch and put out leaves. Some of the markings had worn away, which is how I knew it was paint and not just pattern.

The edges of its body were horny and jagged, and holes had been drilled there for ropes. On the ropes swung a clattering collection of . . . rubbish, I thought. Stones, pieces of wood, different colours and kinds. They served no purpose I could see, save to make noise and weigh the thing down. Although, at half the size of a house, it wouldn't be slowed much.

Amorket was standing right before it, surely within smashing range of those club-like arms. Her wasps were all out, whirling about her in a frenzy, and when they widened their circle, the bracker's head retracted halfway under the shield of its body, flinching. Amorket was shouting at it, telling it to go away, telling it to fight her. The bracker flared its mouthparts back at her, and I saw the circles of skin behind its eyes fuzz in and out. At the edge of my hearing something was tweaking my ears, like some of the sounds the House of our Ancestors made sometimes. Then the animal reared up and stomped its forelegs into the ground, hard enough that I felt the shake of it, and from deep within its body came a single sound, *Brack!*

I thought it was about to turn Amorket into paste, wasps or no wasps, but then it backed off from her, attention turning to us. Erma had a pipe out and was blowing into it, no more than a wheeze of empty air, but the bracker marked her.

Melory darted forwards and pulled at Amorket's arm. The Jalaino woman stood stubbornly for a moment, wasps landing on her and taking off again, blundering at Melory's face and veering away at the last moment.

"What were you thinking?" my sister demanded, but

I knew what Amorket intended. Many an outcast ends up Severed because sometimes a fight is simpler. A fight meant she wouldn't have to deal with me. A fight would help Tsuno, or would end things for Amorket. I reckoned she wouldn't much care which.

The bracker knuckled closer, Amorket forgotten. Its eyes kept turning to me and mine, and it made several mock approaches, shying away each time in a way I knew from animals the world over. *Wrong,* and yet its eyes kept twitching my way, and normally once an animal has decided it doesn't like me, it wastes no time in putting space between us.

Erma was watching it very carefully, reading some truth from it by long experience. She started pulling things from her bag: a sealed gourd, a comb, rope. I saw some of the cords hanging from the edge of the bracker's body looked human-made.

Again that faintest of witterings ghosted from the bracker. Its middle legs unfolded and it picked up each object in turn, rejecting most of them, keeping the rope, testing the texture between its thick fingers. It gave another abortive lunge in my direction, but I and my people stood firm. The digits of its mouth flexed and fidgeted anxiously.

"Scared of you," Erma said quietly. "Doesn't like you one bit."

"Enough to clear out and take its people somewhere else?" I asked her.

"Never seen them like this." Her brow was set in deep lines of thought. "Scared, but . . . it wants something from you, maybe. Like when they're waiting at the posts before we whistle, because they're after a thing we can give them."

Brack! And then it started creeping backwards, one limb at a time, all eyes on us.

It stopped. We stared. It started retreating again, body angled low. It stopped, watching us.

"Follow," Erma said, but really she didn't need to explain it.

~

"We're just going with it, are we?" Kalloi wanted to know, but Erma certainly was, and she didn't seem to care if we went or not. And the bracker, for its part, was warily focused on me and mine. And so we followed it in fits and starts to the bracker village.

Our arrival was heralded by more of those explosive *Brack!* noises. I saw Amorket twitching, the ghostlight dancing about her face in a weird jitter. There were a lot of them.

That was almost the whole of my first impression.

Abruptly there were brackers everywhere between the trees ahead of us, dozens, a hundred, just more and more of them as far as I could see. More than we could ever fight, more than enough to stamp Portruno flat, and do the same to Tsuno tomorrow. Enough to rampage through every village there ever was if they chose. They stomped and reared and *brack*ed, and for a moment I just wanted to run straight away. There was another word the ancestors had that we didn't use anymore, and it was *army*. So many huge, ridgy bodies; so many murderous club feet and thumb-stalked eyes turning our way. So many inhuman thoughts, because Erma had shown us that these were thinking animals, at least a little.

In amongst them were other beasts, things smaller than people but puffed out with long coats of hair, skittering underfoot in packs of eight or ten. I couldn't see much of them beyond the hair, but these must have been the beasts the brackers herded, that gave the fleece Tsuno's hunters made into shirts. I thought the soft, grublike things some brackers cradled with their middle legs were livestock, too, at first, but then guessed the oddly shapeless things were likely young.

And there were houses, too. I didn't mark them as such at first, but then I saw a bracker actually making one. It was nothing more than branches ripped off one tree and then woven round the trunk of another to make a conical roof to shelter under, but that was a bracker house. They made them by rearing up, forefeet against the trunk while those middle arms and their mouth-hand did the weaving.

"Not enough houses," Melory said. She was right, of course. I saw maybe a score of those roofs, nowhere near enough for all the brackers. It made me think I was right that there were just too many of them, and they'd spread out to another home, only it was somewhere that was already home to people. But then she added, "They're injured, some of them."

It wasn't the doctor ghost telling her, but just her being a doctor, inside her head. And she was right, a lot of the brackers looked to have been in a fight. Some of them hobbled about on three good legs, some had dark dents on their backs, or missing eyes. I thought for a moment that the people of Portruno had put up a good fight, but I wasn't seeing spear or knife wounds. Something big and strong had laid into these brackers.

"They fight each other? One village against another?" Because maybe there'd been a bracker war, and these were the losers, driven out of their home.

"Never," Erma told me, but then the beasts had been doing lots of things they never did, so I reckoned she wasn't the authority she used to be.

The one sure thing was that we had their attention.

More and more of them stopped what they were doing and came to stare. Erma played her silent whistle, which I knew must be loud to the brackers, but they were mostly interested in us outcasts, and in Amorket. They came crowding in from all sides, the jagged edges of their big bodies rasping together, lifting their little heads so their two lower eyes could squint at us. Amorket's Furies buzzed angrily, and they shied away a little, so I wondered if the wasps made noises I couldn't hear, too, that the brackers didn't like.

Rubbery fingers tweaked my elbow and I flinched back, finding one of them right next to me. It didn't seem to like what it had touched, though, mouth-hand twisting as though to rid itself of a sour taste. *Brack!* it said, loud enough to deafen me. The call was taken up and repeated across the crowd of them.

"Erma, what do they want?" Melory asked. I heard a little tremble in her voice and knew she was as leery of the mass of animals as I was. Except they hadn't attacked us, no matter what had gone on at Portruno or with the old Lawgiver here.

A bigger bracker was coming through, carrying something beneath its body. Carrying a body beneath its body. A person. I thought it was a corpse at first, but when the bracker laid it down, I heard a whimper from it.

"What have they done to him?" Kalloi murmured, because the man was all over bruises and blood, skin a hundred shades of black and yellow, red and blue. Cuts and grazes and rashes and welts, and yet I thought of any of those brackers attacking someone, and it seemed to me they wouldn't make all those little marks in a fight, they'd smash whole limbs and skulls.

"One of yours," Erma spat. For a moment I couldn't work out what she meant, because of course *we* can't tell. Cut off from the world the ancestors built for their children, we lack the sense of what belongs and what does not. But villagers always know, and so do animals and the rest of the world.

"Nobody I know," Kalloi said, and I was the same. And the more I looked, the less I knew him, because I reckoned I'd recognise this man if I'd ever seen him before. He was very small, and the little of his skin that was unmarked was dead white. He had no hair, and while I've known people who were bald, this man had not a single hair anywhere on his body. He trembled and moaned, sounds that weren't quite words, and his nail-less hands twitched, arms and legs pulled into his body. Everything about him looked weirdly soft and unformed. And, in all this scrutiny, I missed the most obvious thing.

"No Severance," Melory said.

She was right, of course; bruised and ravaged as he was, still that skin was free of one particular stain. The red mixture that marked every one of the Order, and every outcast there ever was, was absent from the man.

"You're sure he's . . . ?"

"Oh, yes. Definitely, yes." She had to force herself to look at him, the same *human-but-not* repulsion as when any villager looked on any of us, the barrier that all the mummery of the Bandage-Men was there to breach.

Then one of the brackers pushed in, looming over the twitching wretch, and its attention was on me. It had something in its hands, proffering it to me. A flat stone with a hole bored in it, I thought, detached from one of its loops of string. A ridgy stone, or maybe something animal, a piece of carapace or horn, because it had that structure to it, built of layers laid down over and over. I took it from the bracker, feeling its dense weight. The edges were jagged, where it had been broken from something larger.

Brack! And everyone was waiting for me to do something, people and brackers, but I didn't know what it was. A rock; a piece of shell.

The bracker stamped a heavy foot right next to the un-marked outcast. He barely reacted. His whimperings and tremblings all arose out of something within him. His eyes saw nothing.

Brack! and it lurched forwards so it could put a mouth-finger on the thing it had given me. Two other fingers reached past and touched my face. I froze. Its touch was slightly sticky. I remembered being told they ate no flesh and hoped that was true.

It ran a finger down where the Severance marked my face. Red, like the carving Erma's Ma had used to call them; like the painting on many of the brackers I could see. I don't know what it meant to them, but it was *something*.

Then there was a commotion from somewhere off in the trees, deeper into the bracker village or perhaps the other side of it. Abruptly the entire mass of them was in motion, ramming into each other, climbing over each other, some heading towards the noise, others away from it. For a brief moment we were an island in that grinding flow, constantly in danger of being crushed on all sides.

Then Melory just dropped, the ghostlight flashing bright as day from the pits of her face. I propped her up. Her one eye was wide, and her lips writhed.

"I hear ghosts!" she got out, clutching at me. "From far away. Ghosts. Ancestors!"

There was a shrill whining sound that bit into my head—I thought it was the wasps, but then one of the bigger brackers had shouldered into us, knocking Kalloi down. The thin sound issued from the vast bulk of its body.

"They hear," Melory got out, before the creature seized

her, rearing up so its middle legs could tear her from my grip and bundle her up. A moment later and it was loping off, out of the frenzied mass, out into the clear trees, Melory clutched to its underside.

VI

I HAD THOUGHT THEY'D be slow, looking at them. The bracker that had Melory was swift as a running man the moment it was out of the press of its fellows. Those huge forelegs pounded down and it swung its body between them, the short hindlimbs nothing but an anchor so it could swing the front pair forwards again. When I tried to pursue, another bracker was in my way, beating at the ground with its clubs and yet not quite wanting to touch me. I shouted at it furiously, waving my metal staff, even striking it across the nearest limb.

"Priest!" Kalloi yelled. I turned to see him trying to haul the hairless outcast with him. The dwarfish creature's flesh deformed under his hands as though it were soft sand, blackening and splitting into runnels of blood. I went back automatically, but a fresh bracker rammed Kalloi aside before recoiling from him. It paused a moment over the hairless man, stamping like a child having a tantrum. I had the sense of conflicting desires within it, driving it into a frenzy.

One bludgeoning fist came down and smashed the

hairless man's body to pulp. I felt as though it could have been Kalloi as easily. The bracker was retreating, jostled by its fellows, shuddering as though the touch of the man's flesh had been toxic. I grabbed Kalloi and hauled him upright. He was white with shock, bloody where the bracker's serrated side had shunted him.

"They're fighting each other!" Amorket shouted over the thunder and scrape. "Fighting, over there." A finger pointed vaguely into the unseen spaces past the trees.

"No!" Erma insisted. "They don't!"

"I don't care," I bellowed at both of them. "Let them slaughter each other. Where's Melory?" I put my face, the Eyes of the Ancestors, right up in Erma's. "Track them, hunter. They broke out of this mess. Follow them!"

But it was easier said than done because there were plenty of shoving, trampling brackers all around us and we couldn't just push our way out. These were the larger ones that had remained behind, and many carrying their unformed young.

Right then I would have butchered the lot of them if I could, but while my nature seemed to be keeping us from being crushed, it wasn't cutting a path through them.

Amorket did that. I will give her that much credit.

Without warning—and she was at my very elbow—she exploded with wasps. Her Furies swarmed us. I felt a searing fire in my arm where one just drove its sting straight into me. Kalloi cried out, too, wrapping himself in his cape to ward them off. I don't think Amorket had any control over them; they just responded to how she felt, and right then she wanted to get out as much as any of us.

The wasps attacked the brackers around us. They dived about the creatures' heads and bounced off their backs like stinging rain. More, they attacked the soft bundles of life the brackers were carrying, stinging the helpless little monsters wherever they could. The seething mass of beasts all around us was suddenly an expanding circle as the creatures tried to escape and protect their larvae.

Amorket moved, and the wasps moved with her, driving fiercely in whatever direction she faced. In such a way we got clear of the brackers; though, by the time we had, the wasps seemed as much of a threat as the animals. I retreated with my people and waited until the Furies had calmed and returned to their homes within the knots of her armour.

By then, Erma had a trail, and I could only hope it was the right bracker we were tracking and not some random beast that had lumbered off into the forest. With no other choice, we were after it, making the best time we could.

~

The bracker had taken Melory downhill, away from Tsuno. I asked Erma what was this way, but all she could say was that it was where the brackers lived, where their villages were, before they came here.

We stopped first when we came to a ploughed-up piece of forest. Trees had been torn up, and those that hadn't bore scars and weeping wounds where something had carved into them on its way through. I reckoned they were all shuffling aside, in their slow way, as the memory of whatever had happened rippled through the forest.

"Portruno," Kalloi said, and the rest of us nodded. Just like the way the earth had been churned up there, just like the path that had led between the wrecked village and the forest.

This doesn't go to where the brackers are, though, I thought, but it didn't mean anything. There were many bracker villages, Erma had said. Possibly they were expanding in all directions, great herds of them driving their paths between the trees. Except even when they had all been panicking and charging around, they hadn't been causing that kind of devastation.

"Erma," I said, after we'd set off again. "Those tracks . . . ?"

"Can't say." Her face was closed up, unreadable. "Too much gone past, can't see any prints at all."

"Are we gaining on Melory?"

"Can't say."

And then we ran out of forest.

We'd come to a dip in the ground, a fold between hills, and here we rejoined that devastation, except it was still being enacted. Even as we arrived there was the splintering snap of a tree being pushed over, and the whole dell had been ground clear, broken trunks and branches, spiralling sprays of leaves, all piled up on either side.

Things moved across the barren ground, grinding through the mud. They looked like rocks, save they were all roughly the same shape, like a great stone hood curving back on itself at the rear. They ploughed across the earth, raising a wake of mud and ravaged roots. Where they met resistance, they just braced themselves and shoved, and eventually the stone or tree just gave, undermined and turned aside.

Melory's voice, high and clear over the grind and crack of the stone-things, was like a knife jammed in me. She was calling my name.

We found her in the middle of the scar of ravaged land. The bracker had dragged her there and was still holding on to her arm with one of its stubby hands. She kicked at it and wrenched, but the creature's grip was strong enough to leave great round bruises on her arm.

I was running before I knew it, leaping over the torn earth brandishing my staff. The bracker reared back, yanking Melory half off her feet, slamming its clubs down to turn me aside. Erma was shouting but right then I had no time for her or her mystery.

The head of my staff danced before its eyes, and then I had Kalloi on my left and Illon on my right, shouting and waving their arms, throwing stones. The bracker twittered at us and reared again, shoving towards me with one arm without actually striking me. All around us the stone-things went about their destructive business. We shouted and Erma blew her pipe and it *bracked*. And now I wonder if it was demanding answers or trying to provide them.

What I did see was that the bracker had let Melory go.

It backed off from us, head low, side-eyes weaving about. It made a noise I hadn't heard from them before, a kind of liquid gurgling. Erma stopped still, face set.

I was in the middle of asking what that meant when it went for one of the stone-things, just bounded off sideways and slammed into the thing's shell with both clubbed fists. I saw a crack flower from the impact and suddenly understood what the brackers had been showing me before: the piece of ridgy stone had been a shard of shell.

Then the stone thing fought back.

What had seemed no more than a boulder grubbing its way through the dirt lifted up into angry motion on long, pinkish legs, doubling its height. It was fast, too, dancing back on four limbs and striking out with the front two, so that the pair of monsters threatened and beat at each other with blows that would have crushed any of us. I rushed to Melory, who was on the ground. I thought the bracker had hurt her, but she was clutching at her head and the ghostlight pulsed there in odd rhythms.

"Voices," she got out. "There are ghosts here!"

I was still trying to get her to her feet, but the others drew back from her. Even Severed from the villages, there's something about ghosts that commands reverence. Even having been to the House of our—

"Ancestors," as though Melory was reading my mind.

"Attack!" Amorket's high shriek, and I thought for a moment it was just her being her, like facing off against the bracker. Then I had a moment to look around and saw things had all gone horribly wrong.

All the stone-things were in furious motion. And they weren't stone-things, not when those long legs came out and they were flurrying over the turned earth towards the bracker. They were coming to the aid of their kin, fast as running men. One of them almost trampled Erma, who was trying to get the bracker's attention. It was Kalloi who dragged her clear.

The bracker whirled, lashing out at them, shrilling, making that gargling sound again. The strike of its clubs against their shells was like the retorts of thunder. For a moment the shell-creatures were hesitating, kept back by its sheer fury. Then they began baiting it, each one attacking the bracker's back when it was turned to them, backing off when it spun to face them.

By then we were trying to get away, me hauling Melory and Kalloi dragging Erma. Except the stone-things were between us and the trees, and they were noticing us, now. They high-stepped close, tilted and peered. I saw nests of eyes protruding and retracting at the lip of their shells. Under the arching limbs, a hideous mouth sucked and slapped.

Melory jerked in my hands, and I saw one of them was pawing at her foot. I hit it with my staff, and it recoiled, from me rather than the force of the blow, because the contact was almost nothing. They were trying to get to Erma, too, and Amorket, but we of the Order were . . .

I was thinking that we were abhorrent, as we were to any animal, but it wasn't like that. They didn't shy away from us as the brackers had. They pushed past us, tried to shove us out of the way to get to their prey, but . . . politely, almost. Insistently, but they could have trampled us flat and they didn't.

And yet they were monstrously strong, and we couldn't stop them, could only dance around Melory and Erma for so long. Then one of them got at Amorket and knocked her down—nobody had really cared to be her guard, in all honesty. I thought that was it for her, and perhaps we could get out while she had their attention. I reckoned without the gifts Jalaino had given her, though.

Her Furies boiled out of her armour, mad as their namesake, just as they had amongst the brackers. They attacked whatever was closest, and that meant the stone-thing that had floored her. I saw them dart and lance into its pinkish-grey flesh, and the creature recoiled, that hideous mouth gaping to show a host of writhing limbs and teeth within it. It made a sound, a sickening sound. I felt ill just hearing it, though I couldn't understand why right then.

The expanding ring of wasps washed over us, and all the shelled beasts were rocking and lurching away, or hunkering down so that the rims of their shells were flush with the earth.

I had Melory moving immediately. Her ghostlight was so bright I could have read by it, and she seemed completely lost to the world. The others were right on my heels.

When we got to the trees, I heard another sound, so shrill it felt like someone boring a hole in my skull. I looked back and saw the bracker torn bodily apart, each limb hauled in a different direction by one of the stone-things. Erma's cry of shock came right after.

~

After we had caught our breath, we found a vantage that gave us a better view, the knocking and groaning of the stone-things echoing hollowly to us. Below us, where once was unbroken canopy, a scar curved out through the forest. Stone-things were moving there, a dozen of them, some far larger than we'd seen before. They ground forwards at their inexorable pace, ploughing earth already thoroughly churned up by the passage of their fellows. Some curved off to the edge of the scar to widen it, pushing over trees and turfing up great stones. Their strength seemed limitless. Nothing could stand against them, and their concerted effort seemed to have a dreadful purpose to it. Not the grazing of beasts, but creatures acting in concert to widen their road, just as the villagers at Orovo had made paths around their village. The scar went as far as the eye could see, off until the trees consumed it, until the heavy, greenish air obscured it.

"Brackers live over that way." Erma's shaking hand could have meant anywhere, but we understood. Brackers didn't live there anymore, I guessed. These stone-things had carved a path through their villages, broken their houses as they'd destroyed Portruno. Driven the brackers before them until the creatures had ended up squatting on the doorstep of their human neighbours.

We spent a night under the trees on our way back to Tsuno. Kalloi was already pale from more than just shock, by then, shivering by our fire as Melory tried to help him. She was still trying to work out what she had experienced. Some ghosts, she said. Or perhaps something like ghosts, as the ancestors were like ghosts. Something that could talk to the ghost part of her.

For me, I didn't sleep much. That sound the stone-thing made still haunted me, its cry when the wasps stung it. I had heard the ancestors speak in their own way, those words that are like and unlike the ones we use. The sounds the stone-thing made had struck my ear like their words. As though human words had come from that ghastly gaping mouth. "No, no," my ears had heard, and, "Mother!"

Interlude

The Sister Colony: Part Two

"**WE CAUGHT ONE,**" Lena Dal said. "Right up against the perimeter."

Bain stared dully at her. "Perimeter," he echoed. Because there wasn't a perimeter. They were up on a scarp slope, the sea still a grey-brown line on the horizon. A half-dozen emergency quarantine domes linked together, like a child's imitation of the research base they'd abandoned. All they had left.

"Are you listening to me?" Lena demanded. "We caught one. A snail. It was right there."

"Tell everyone we . . ." The thought was so morbidly depressing Bain couldn't quite enunciate it. *I'm the director,* he told himself, though director of *what* was a fair question. "We have to move again." Farther inland, towards the line of those scale-trunked, twisted trees; towards the distant landing site they hadn't been able to contact, the main expedition that hadn't even come looking for them.

There had been a flier, just the once. It had passed over the beach and doubtless seen the wreckage. They had waited for it to swing back and make a determined search for survivors, but it had never returned. And yes, there had been harsh words when Bain's team had schismed from the main expedition, rejecting their plans for the future of the colony. He wouldn't believe that was the reason, though. They were just desperate. He knew how that felt. This world was death, and doubtless one look had been enough to assure them that the sister expedition was gone. It was a mindset this planet cultivated. Nothing would ever turn out well. It was cursed.

And now they were going to have to move again.

"Are you even listening to me, Bain?" Lena was shaking, ever so slightly.

"Perimeter. Snail. Have to move," he mumbled.

"Bain, we're a kilometre from the littoral zone here. There *are* no snails. It's not their habitat. But this one was amongst the tents. It had taken the water purifier apart, just laid the pieces out, eaten some of them. That could have been one of *us*, Bain."

And it could. Because they'd sent a drone back to the lab complex to look for other survivors. Bain had seen the recording where two snails had been organising the various pieces of Orindo Snapper, technician. They'd eaten parts of him, though some of the biotechs were saying it wasn't actually eating. Other parts had been placed in a circular pattern, organised. *Filed.*

"So we . . . move. What do you want me to say?"

"They have come *after* us," Lena spelled out for him. "They have come way outside their normal range, for us."

He tried a level stare, the sort of expression a serious director would have. "Are you saying the snails want *revenge?*"

"Revenge?" Lena snapped. "*I* want revenge, Bain. I want to murder every last one of the bastards. I'm saying that there's some damn thing we have they want. We have their *attention,* Bain."

Something terrible was building up inside him. "You're saying we're going to be . . . hunted to the end of the Earth . . . by *snails?*" And it was a laugh, and he couldn't stop it. Even to his ears it sounded grotesque, the braying of a dying animal.

"Bain!" She looked like she wanted to slap him. He wouldn't have blamed her. "Shay thinks the . . . the big one's on the move."

That killed the laugh. They hadn't seen the hill-sized snail since they abandoned the base. They didn't even have enough drones to go look for it, because the trundling remotes just kept not coming back. The image of the colossal thing wrenching itself from the earth recurred to him. *And can it move as fast as the others?* In his imagination, of course it could. It could coast over the landscape, light and vast as a zeppelin, its mass returning to it only in the moment it put its feet down to obliterate them.

"We have to fight," Lena told him. "We've caught this one. We can take it apart, for a proper examination. Find a way to poison them, something they don't like. I've already asked the biotech team to . . ." She stuttered to silence, because of course she was here to get his rubber stamp of authority on just such an action. Bain just waved it all by. *One more decision I don't have to make.*

When she came shouting for him, three hours later, he assumed the worst: an army of snails on the horizon, the entire slope beneath them just one more alien monster a mile across. There was something unfamiliar in Lena's haggard face, though. It was excitement.

"You've got to come and see," she gabbled at him. "You've got to brace yourself. It's . . . not good, Bain. It's horrible. But . . . the implications! You've got to see for yourself."

So he went, and he saw for himself, and it was horrible. But at the same time it was hope.

VII

KALLOI DIED THE NIGHT after we got back to Tsuno.

It was the blood. He got torn up when the brackers went mad. When, perhaps, the stone-things turned up at the far side of their village, and they were fighting. We wrap ourselves in these bandages because the world is poison to us, in a way that actual poison is not. That is the backwards way we live. The things that are made to be dangerous—venom, savage beasts—are no terror to us, but mundane things that no villager would worry about can be death. That poison world got into Kalloi's wound. When we got him back, he was already shivering, his skin livid, feverish. He was babbling, and Melory did her best but it was not enough. Before the sun rose, Kalloi had fought the stuff of the world that was inside him, and lost. We of the Order took him and burned him, rather than the village way of returning someone to the earth. The things of the earth will not decay us.

It was not the first time. In fact, it was a common thing. If a wound could be washed, with boiled water, then most likely the patient would live. Or sometimes the wound swelled angrily but the fever broke, and they lived. Sometimes a life could be saved with the loss of a limb, a second severance to cut away the poisoned part. It was a reaction, Melory said. The thing that killed us was not even the world-stuff itself, but the way our bodies could not abide it. Our blood, our flesh, fought so fiercely against the touch of every part of this world that we consumed ourselves, a man who burns his house down to drive out the vermin that had crept into it.

Illon was very drawn. She had come with Kalloi and me, seen all we had seen. He had died, and it might have been her. It was her first true lesson about life in the Order.

"All we can do is remember," I told her. "I've told you the Ancestors had their way of setting down what they knew, their *writing*. There is a wall in their House where we place the names of all who come to the Order and pass on, as we all shall. Kalloi's name shall join them. We die, Illon. But we live longer than we would alone and Severed."

I watched her carefully. This was often the moment you can see whether someone will thrive in the Order. She didn't rail or complain. Instead she looked me in the eyes and said, "What can we do?" And she meant revenge; she meant doing the job we'd been called here for.

"We are going before the Lawgiver again," I told her.

"But I think we will go to war."

~

The boy Lawgiver got a collection of Tsuno's more re-spected people together to hear what we had to say. Old men and women, mostly, confused and uncertain, shoul-ders not strong enough for the load they were having to bear. Looking over them, I saw the limitations of village life. They'd lived all their days with the ghosts telling them how to do it. They hadn't had to make decisions about any-thing important. A bad harvest, a sickness, a shortage, the appropriate ghost would have the answer. And I remem-bered thinking just this, when Melory finally brokered the compact that led to the Bandage-Men and our mystery. We made things better. We solved problems they didn't know they had, because any problems the ghosts didn't address just became part of the way life was. And suddenly the Ban-dage-Men were fighting their beasts and taking their out-casts. And passing word from one village to another, and though that seemed the least of what we do, ten years has shown me it's actually the biggest change of all. As the Or-der grows and prospers, villages will become more and more used to being able to speak to one another at will, and even the ghosts will start to figure us into their advice, and the world will become better.

But right then we were on the raw frontier, and that great change for the best was still just ripples moving out from Orovo and the House of our Ancestors. It hadn't reached Tsuno, particularly. And Tsuno had a problem I wasn't sure how to help with.

As chief hunter, Erma was right there when Melory and I stood before the Lawgiver. I saw she wanted to control the words. She didn't want us to talk about her mystery, but more than that, it was the brackers. She didn't war with the brackers. She'd lived her whole life a secret way that let Tsuno, all unknowing, use the brackers just like we want the villages to use us. To make things better, even if the ghosts and most of the people never realised.

If we stood before the Lawgiver and said, we must go and fight the brackers, burn their houses, drive them out, they'd do it. We would lead, but they would come after. And people won against animals, usually. Although the brackers were very strong, and also very smart. I didn't much fancy the idea of going to war with them, if I were honest with myself. And yet what we were actually going to propose seemed worse.

Melory set it out for them. If it were just a matter of fighting brackers, it would be me, because that's what they know I'm for. Because it was more complicated than that, better Melory took the lead.

She told them what we learned in brief, terse sentences. She had been up all night with Kalloi, and I saw the strain on her. It was hard for a villager to feel the death of one of ours, even if that villager was Melory, but the doctor ghost felt the death of a patient, and that let her open the door to grief a crack.

I heard her say the brackers were here because other things had come to where the brackers lived. She described the stone-things, which were strange and new to everyone. She said the stone-things were making war on the brackers. Without ever mentioning Erma's mystery, she said we should see if we can push the stone-things away, and then maybe the brackers would go back to their places and leave Tsuno alone. The Lawgiver would do anything she told him to, I thought, because the ghost had nothing.

After that, we talked amongst ourselves. The stone-things didn't quite react to us like animals normally do, but they didn't seem to want to attack us. We should make best use of that, therefore. We should take our strength here and go to where they are clearing the land, go deep into their place and see what we can see. Worst come to worst, we could take strong beams and overturn them to attack the soft parts underneath, or heavy stones to break their shells. There was a pattern and a plan to the way they were moving, though, which might mean that there was some vital point, a stone-thing leader perhaps, a hatchery we could destroy. A village of many people is stronger than just many people each on their own. Yet a village has ghost-bearers: threaten them, and the strength of the village is paralysed. Sharskin knew that, and he held a whole village helpless while they outnumbered our people twenty to one. Not my proudest moment, and yet a lesson worth learning. If the stone-things had leaders . . .

Or ghost-bearers . . .

I gave my followers the plan. Some wanted to fight the brackers instead, for Kalloi, but they would do what I told them. I instructed them to spend the day preparing to fight. Sharpen their knives, gather stones for their slings.

"You must do the same for the Tsuno folk," I suggested to Melory, after. "If it is war, we will need them, too, backing us up." We would be the vanguard, doing the fighting, but if the villagers could come after, finishing the wounded among the stone-things, breaking their houses if they had them, that would free us to keep pushing forwards.

"The Lawgiver can do that," Melory said. "You'll need me. Because of the ghosts."

"Tell me about the ghosts." Because when she was overcome by them, in the middle of the stone-things . . .

I had only seen her like that once before, and it was the first time she came to the House of our Ancestors, when Sharskin caught her. The ancestors tried to talk to her ghost, her expert system, and it nearly drove her mad before she mastered them.

She nodded, when I mentioned it. "Incompatible systems," she said. "But it was close, maddeningly close. I could hear words . . . like the ancestors talking, almost."

And then a wasp flung itself past my face and I flinched away, looking round for Amorket. She was at my shoulder again, in that way of hers, but this time her focus was on Melory.

"You hear them, too."

We looked at her warily.

"The voices," she said. "You hear the voices. Many and one. Speaking terrible things." She was looking gaunter than before, and I was grimly sure it was because her personal hive was breeding ever more wasps from her, consuming her even as it urged her on.

"I do . . ." Melory said slowly, and I braced myself in case this was something Amorket would treat as punishable by death.

Instead, the Champion seemed to sag within her armour. "I thought it was just me," she whispered, and I interpreted that as, *I thought I was going mad.* "I hear the Furies all the time, but when we were there . . ."

"Your wasps . . . talk to you?" Melory frowned.

"They tell me where they are, what they are doing, always, all of them all the time," Amorket confirmed hollowly, and then, in a weird singsong voice, "*Telemetry targeting requesting refuel reservoir exhausted percentage recalculating recalculating.*" Her jaw snapped shut. Melory was staring at her, wide-eyed.

"Can you talk back?" she asked.

"They don't listen to me," Amorket said sullenly. I remembered her shouting at the bracker and wondered if it had actually been her Furies she'd been yelling at. "They . . . they know me. They feel with me. I am angry, they are angry." Though her wasps never seemed less than angry to me. "I want to fight, they fight; I triumph, they triumph. I am calm, they . . . but it is so hard. I cannot find the calm in me." Her face spasmed and the wasps boiled out from her armour and crawled about her, as though jealous that she was talking about them.

Melory blinked. "Handry, Amorket and I need to come with you, when you go to where the stone-things are. I know that'll make things more difficult, but you need to protect us, and I need to . . . gather information, use my ghost to scout."

"If it gives us a choice other than just going to war," I agreed. I remembered the stone-things killing the bracker. Not hard to imagine a person being ripped apart in the same way.

"And I need to speak to the House." She was already on her feet and heading towards the Tsuno tree and its hive, which would amplify her words and pass them on.

~

The next morning Erma had left before us, on her own. She was going to the brackers, I knew, and I didn't like the idea that she was out there following her own path, which might clash with the Lawgiver or with me. If it came to Tsuno or her brackers I had no doubt she'd fight for her village, but she was trying to save both. I wasn't sure what she might do, what seemed a good idea to her right up until the moment it went wrong.

She was outside our control or knowledge, though, so Melory and I mustered the Order and we all set out ahead of first light, heading into the wilds. Our path would detour around the bracker village, heading for the ragged wound in the trees the stone-things had made. Depending on what happened it might come to war with the brackers instead, but I didn't want to think about that just then.

Melory was very quiet for most of the journey, walking in the midst of us to make sure nothing from the forest tried to go for her. Amorket trailed us as usual, and I kept my eye on her.

The stone-things had cleared more trees when we came to their scar. They had bared a whole valley that led sloping off downwards to the northwest, working out from what I thought was a great rocky hill at first. Looking down the slope at them, we saw plenty of their curved shells dotting the barren ground. Some were still, others worked at shunting rocks and trunks. A couple were . . . well, I wasn't sure what they were doing, save that they were using their rubbery fistfuls of mouthparts to pick up and play with the detritus their progress had left behind, making patterns with it, as they had at Portruno with the bodies of the dead.

"Is there some secret in that?" I asked Melory. "Like the writing of the ancestors?"

"If so, I can't read it." She had her eyes almost closed anyway.

"You hear them?"

She nodded.

Illon pushed forwards hesitantly. "Do the shells have ghosts in them?"

Melory shook her head, eyes entirely closed now. "Ghosts," she said in her teaching voice, "are something made by our ancestors to help the villages. It's not as though ghosts could . . . get lost from a hive and seek out a new home, but . . ." But she didn't know, was the obvious answer.

"That's what they talk to." Amorket had walked a few yards along the slope and was staring over at the hill. Even as I went over, some part of my mind was picking at that: a hill planted down lopsidedly in the middle of the valley as though it had fallen from the sky like the House of our Ancestors once did. It looked out of place; it loomed higher than our own vantage point, and the stream that ran along the valley floor pooled around the foot of it, its natural course obstructed.

The stone-things were busy around it, and in and out of a crack in the hillside. Except the crack seemed weirdly regular, as though someone had just lifted the edge of the hill's base up into a peak there, like I might with the hem of a cloak.

"They talk," Amorket said. I could see the dots of her Furies as they ranged through the air towards the hill. At the same time the shape of that hill was nagging at my mind, as was the way the earth had been disturbed in a vast furrow stretching back from its base.

Illon voiced the thought before I could, and perhaps I was too leery of being thought a fool.

"It's one of them," she said. And of course that was impossible, but at the same time, the moment she said it, we could all see it. It was large enough that the regular stone-things could pass in and out of it easily, dominating them and the landscape both. We did not see it move, but the track of its progress overnight was plain to see. The stone-things had brought their house with them, a living house that moved on its own, just like the House of our Ancestors.

"She's right," Melory pronounced. "They talk to it."

"Talk how?"

"Like the ghosts talk to the tree. They have ears that catch invisible sounds, sounds that don't pass through the air like our words, but are carried by..." She grimaced. "It's like there are invisible rivers, and when I use my ghost to speak to the House, the river carries my words there, because of what was built in my head. Which means these stone-things have something within them that is the same."

"Where does this get us?" I was staring at the hill, trying to imagine it moving. The edge of it tearing out of the mud, vast finger-legs beneath stretching themselves...

"What if we could use it to talk to them? When the bracker attacked one, the others all swarmed in," Melory went on thoughtfully. "I heard it call them and tell them it was hurt." A sidelong look at Amorket. "They're like *her* and her Furies, always linked by this talking. So I've been thinking, what if we shout?" She saw I didn't understand her. "Shout, Handry. Shout so the others can't hear it when it calls. Flood the river with our own words."

"Won't they come because they hear us shouting?" Illon asked.

Melory was grinning now. "If we shout just right, then nobody will hear anything. Our words meet their words and run into them, so nothing gets down the river at all."

~

We picked our ambush carefully, finding a wall of the valley the stone-things had carved up until there was a good straight drop down to the churned mud below. Melory picked out our target, a stone-thing engaged in shoving and dredging the loose stones and fractured wood towards the valley's edge. Leaving Graf in charge, I and a half dozen of our company descended, carrying stout branches as big as we could handle. We crept close to the thing as it ground along, and it paused for a moment before moving on, turned a little to give us space.

The first of the wasps looped past, almost bouncing off the stone-thing's shell, and then the air was busy with them, dancing about the stone-thing. They didn't sting, but just swung about it, crawled over it, the air heavy with their buzzing.

The stone-thing stopped moving and a shudder went through it. That was the sign that Melory's plan was working, I hoped. She said she would use Amorket's wasps to amplify her words, so that instead of a single voice, the air around the stone-thing would be thronging with an unheard chorus, taking up all the space in that invisible river, making it impossible for the beast to speak to its fellows.

The creature lurched, rising half up onto its legs and stumbling before dropping back down. Abruptly it seemed confused, blind to the world and not knowing which way to go. That was our signal and we rushed forwards, planting our branches in the dirt at the shell's base and levering it towards the high side of the valley. It was huge and strong, and if it had just been shove against shove, we'd never have moved it, but it was confused and unsteady. I could read a human panic in its movements at suddenly being severed from its fellows. Every time it tried to go another way, we dug in our stakes and deflected it. Every time it veered towards the cliff, we pushed it on. Occasionally we saw the black dots of eyes weaving from beneath the shell, trying to understand what was going on, and we kicked at them, struck them with our branches. We harried the thing mercilessly because, if it had been given a chance to recover, it could have crushed us easily.

Then its leading edge rammed the carved side of the valley, bringing a shower of stones and dirt. I heard the call from above and jammed my branch into the earth, anchoring it as deep as possible to pin the cumbersome shell between it and the wall. My fellows were doing likewise and then we were all running clear.

Up above, Graf's people had their own levers and were prying the biggest rock they could find over the edge. I heard Amorket's shriek of triumph as it went over. She must have been in the forefront of the push, burning the strength the Furies infused her with.

I half expected the stone to just bounce from the stone-thing's curved shell, leaving nothing but a pale scrape. Instead the missile led with a jagged edge that shattered the creature into twenty pieces and exposed torn pinkish flesh beneath.

We swarmed forwards. I was looking for . . . I can't say what I was looking for, but perhaps my imagination had conceived of something like the angular devices of the ancestors, tucked under the thing's shell. Instead it was all a mass of pinkish grey, shapeless now the shell had gone, some firm as muscle, other parts running like jelly. We got our branches and tried to pull it apart, to find whatever it was inside that spoke.

Abruptly it opened up. There was a chamber within it, a hollow heart to the beast. We exposed it to the air and then recoiled with cries of horror.

In the centre of the stone-thing, we found something. Curled up on itself, broken by the stone's impact, there was no mistaking the form of a man.

Interlude

The Sister Colony: Part Three

ORINDO SNAPPER WAS WAVING at him.

Or that was the first impression Bain's overdrugged and sleep-deprived brain gave him.

The snail was still alive, although they'd peeled the thing out of its shell and partially anatomised it. Which meant that, in some weird remnant way, Orindo Snapper was still alive, too. Despite the fact that they'd all seen his head and various chunks of him being passed back and forth by the snails.

It was Orindo's arm, his left arm. DNA had confirmed ownership and Bain guessed they could even have taken its fingerprints if anyone had a particularly forensic turn of mind.

It was attached to the snail. Specifically, it had been grafted, if that was the word, to the lining of the interior chamber of the creature they'd caught, the one that'd come sniffing around their camp. There was quite a selection of junk in that fleshy sac, much of it from their abandoned research base. All of it was set into the thick walls of the cavity. Not just sitting there, either. On the other side of a clear dividing panel, Geordi Gownt the biologist was talking them through it as the medical remote continued the dissection.

Vivisection, Bain corrected himself, watching the ripple and twitch of Orindo's fingers.

"This inner chamber . . ." Geordi was a cadaverously thin man now, haggard and grey, reacting to their current state of emergency even worse than Bain. "The whole organism is . . . organised about it." His words came in an irregular ebb and flow, at the whim of tides of fatigue. "The structures surround it . . . far more complex than just storage as we'd . . . as we thought. Perhaps it evolved from . . . but now, we think, we think it's a way of experiencing the world, we . . ." There was no *we.* They couldn't spare a whole team on the investigation, just him.

"A sense organ," Bain prompted. "They, what, take stuff in to feel it out and taste it?"

"More, more than that," Georgi insisted, seemed to forget he was talking for a moment, then pressed on. "This tissue here, this is what carries reactive and impulsive . . . impulses around the body. Nerve tissue analogues, though the biochemistry is . . . incompatible with ours. Obviously. Native life here, it's . . . less centralised.

And from what we observed before we . . . came out here, from what the main team observed, the more complex the behaviours, the more distributed the neurology. Opposite of what you'd expect in Earth life. Whole body a brain, almost. This species, it's as spread out as we've seen, but more . . ."

"Just get to the damned *point,* Geordi!" Lena fairly shouted at him.

"This is . . ." He looked hurt. "This is the point, what I'm trying to tell you . . ."

"The membrane of the chamber, you said," she drove on relentlessly.

Orindo kept waving, posthumously. Bain fought down the urge to wave back.

"Well yes, it does seem to, does appear that some remarkable . . ." Something seemed to sharpen in Geordi's face and manner. "Director, the membrane serves as a permeable biochemical interface with the world, a profoundly catholic one. We've tried introducing it to a variety of substances, including many that are toxic to the native life here." Meaning commonplace Earth substances, Bain suspected. "The membrane has adapted to serve as an . . . interface, perhaps that's the . . . it can . . ." They were losing him again. His hand trembled and the arms of the medical remote halted, fail-safes cutting in.

Lena took up the slack. "Bain, we came here because there seemed more give in the oceanic biochemistry, so we thought we might be able to adapt it to our needs more easily than the terrestrial biomes the main team is working with. And we've found the give, or at least our best example of it. These snails are equipped to take on an incredible range of habitats—temperature, chemical gradients, pressure. We think that there must be a huge variation in conditions across their undersea range, and rather than speciate to specialise in particular niches, they're the ultimate generalists. This organ, this cavity of theirs, it can alter its composition to make use of whatever it comes across. Which is probably why they can break from the water so easily. But the same ability means they can bridge the gap to us."

Bain stared at that forlorn hand. "What am I even looking at?" he complained. "A sense organ, you said. So this is it . . . investigating Snapper?"

"We're a component of a new environment, something biochemically distinct and alien, but they've evolved to encompass anything they come across, and that dumb adaptation has done what all our research has failed to achieve," Lena told him. "This is the key, Bain. This is what we take back to the main team, when we can finally get a channel open to hail them. The goddamned *snails* have done the hard work for us. We can build on what we learn here. We're going to live, Bain. The colony's going to live."

"Well then . . ." All too big, too much, overwhelming. "We need access to the ship, servitors, more samples. We need that open channel."

"We need more snails," Lena finished for him. "I'll get a team together and go hunting, see if any others have come up the beach after us."

She was almost joyous as she marched off.

~

Geordi Gownt stood in the clean room after the pair of them had gone. Not exactly clean, not now, not with various snail fluids all over it. Clean in the sense it kept the mess in one place. The medical remote was still paused, waiting for him to pick up where he'd left off. The snail quivered and spasmed beneath its poised knives, showing no signs of dying just yet.

He hadn't been able to say what he'd wanted to say, but that was more and more a feature of his life, here out on the frayed edge of human existence. The words wouldn't come, or came lumped together so densely that the pressure twisted his meaning into obscurity.

A sense organ, they'd said, but that hadn't been what he meant, quite. Yes, the snails used the lining of their internal cavity to experience the world, just as a human might use their hands to feel something out. And yes, that investigation of whatever objects it ingested was conducted at biochemical arm's length, and in a way that led to rapid change and adaptation of the lining so that the snail could safely handle whatever it took in. Geordi didn't think you *could* poison them, which had been Lena Dal's original instructions. They probably had the mother of all immune systems, too, or the local equivalent. But none of that quite explained the grafting.

The late Orindo Snapper's arm was not just set into the wall of the cavity. There was a permeable connection between human tissue and snail. The conductive fibres of the not-mollusc's body had, via the adaptable cavity membrane, meshed with the dead nervous tissue of Snapper and revivified it, taken it over. And of course that didn't mean the snail would be touch-typing or shaking anyone by the hand any time soon. Nonetheless, the random twitches of those moribund fingers were being triggered by impulses originating within the alien creature, and Geordi couldn't find any sign of ongoing decay in the hand.

Which should have him ferociously excited. It was arguably the medical discovery of the century. They could isolate the membrane and use it to preserve human organs and parts perhaps forever. And he hadn't even mentioned the facility to Bain and Lena, because it wasn't what was on his mind.

What he'd discovered, in examining the boundary between human and alien flesh, was the ongoing changes to the snail's fine structure, spreading out from that connection. Similar, lesser, changes could be tracked from everything else it had implanted into that cavity wall. There was some manner of mediated dialogue between the physiology of the organism and whatever it ingested and stored.

Geordi stared at the dying snail, trying to pull all these strands of thought together. As though the collection of findings the creature had taken in was not just being felt out and examined but was being incorporated into the entity's very workings. *Becoming part of its mind,* came the sleep-deprived song in his head. *The snail has Orindo on the brain.* It didn't have a mind, of course, or even a brain. And yet he watched the flowerings of new structures and new complexity spread into the snail, fast enough to be visible, fanning out from where it had latched on to the human arm. He watched and felt a curious sense of dread.

VIII

A SMALL MAN, HIS skin so pale I felt the sun had never touched it before now. Hairless, toothless (I saw, as his jaw was smashed). And yet a man.

Like the brackers' captive, save ours was already dead. And I remembered how that unfortunate's pasty skin had been bruised and broken, ruptured and bloody every which way. I thought the brackers had beaten him, before. Looking at this exhumed corpse, I felt that to touch that skin would be like plunging my fingers into mud. And he was not separate. He was not apart from the thing that had contained him. Probably the blood and other injuries the brackers' captive had borne had concealed the signs, but we could clearly see that there were places where his body and the slick grey-pink flesh of the stone-thing touched without boundary between them. A shuddering of death in one rippled through the other without division.

Everyone was staring at the body, but I stood and looked past them, out at the muddy waste where the stone-things dragged their shells. I saw them anew, picturing encysted within each one a curled-up human form.

Melory was kneeling by the ruin of flesh. She had found other things that had been fitted around the man's body within its womb. They were lumpy, irregular, as though they had wept out of the stone-thing's flesh like pus from a wound, and then coagulated.

"I think," she said slowly, "this was what I heard talking."

"It's a ghost?" The pieces she had looked a little like metal, but only a little.

"A ghost's mouth," she told me, and then Illon had called out, because there were other stone-things coming over. When that mouth had ceased speaking, they had heard the silence.

They didn't just crawl towards us in that slow, relentless way of theirs. They were up on their long legs, high striding their way over the ground. I saw a dense fist of mouthparts there hiding a palm full of teeth and hooks and rasps. It had been terrible before, but how much more so now I could picture the cramped cadaver at its heart! I felt a revulsion to my very bones, and wondered if this was how *we* looked to the villagers, something unnatural given a final edge by the fact that it looked *like us*.

I ran forwards, holding my arms out, staff held high. I was ready to beat a quick retreat if I needed to, but the nearest stone-thing veered off and then came back, the fingers of its mouth waving before my face but not touching me. Black button eyes peered at me from the shell's rim, but I felt it was using some sense other than mere looking. It knew I was there, and it knew me for something apart from the world. Not the instinctive aversion of a beast, nor yet the antipathy of a human being. Something new. It was, I think, curious.

Melory, and the Tsuno scouts, they'd all seen the bracker's prisoner and known him for Severed, though he'd had none of the mark on him. I would have to tread through the implications of that when I was out of the stone-thing's shadow.

More were coming, and they knew Melory was there, and Amorket, too. They kept trying to bully past us to get to prey they could understand. And yet we stood in their way, shifting, shouting, even pushing at their shells or striking them with sticks. We were confusing whatever sense they relied on. They couldn't work out what we were. Or else they were thinking it over, and any moment they'd come to a decision and crush us.

"Melory," I said. "You need to go. Go back to Tsuno. Take Amorket and run."

We had been forced away from the shattered stone-thing, and now one of its fellows had discovered it. Its mouthparts and feelers pattered across the dead flesh, human and beast, and then a sound came from it, not a word, but near to a word. As though a tongueless man was trying to give voice to his grief. Abruptly all the stone-things nearby were moving with a greater purpose, more and more insistent as they tried to push past us. I felt they knew villagers were close, but they couldn't quite know where, as though they had the scent of them but nothing more. Our presence was confusing them.

"Go," I said again.

"What about you?"

"I'm not in danger like you are. We'll cover for your escape. We'll see what else is here. Maybe there are eggs we can break or food stocks we can ruin." Our standard tactics for driving out beasts, which surely wouldn't be sufficient here. I wanted to say she should tell Tsuno what we'd found out, but what would the villagers do with such knowledge? She would tell the House, though, and perhaps the ancestors had some memory of what we faced, or had a weapon we could turn on them. "Just go," and then a stone-thing knocked me down, not intending to but impatient to get to what it knew was there.

I thought Amorket would stay, stubborn as she was, but when Melory scrambled back up the slope she followed, leaving only those of us in the Original Condition to face the stone-things.

Except they would not face us, but wanted to follow

Melory out of the valley, and probably all the way to Tsuno. I knew we had to prevent that, and so we got to work. We started with noise, and we beat on their shells with sticks. Then, when they were reaching the top of the valley side, we got our beams and branches and levered them up, all of us bending our backs against each one to upend it and send it down. I'd hoped to see them rocking on their tops, legs waving in the air, but they righted themselves with dismaying speed, and then one of them kicked Illon, knocking her onto her back and winding her.

It was above her immediately, arched legs a cage around her. She didn't scream, but kicked at its fleshy underside, and I saw a mouth gape there. Not a mouth, not quite. An opening to that inner chamber, the house of the pallid men.

I dashed forwards and seized Illon by the wrist, hauling her out from under the creature's shadow. I was too late, really. I saw what I'd far rather not. The orifice in the thing's underside had yawned open and peering out through it I met eyes set in a dead white face, devoid of expression, nail-less hands questing blindly out towards where Illon had been, slack mouth mumbling. I didn't want to hear what it had to say.

We kept moving, not anywhere but in circles, and the stone-things crawled, now slowly, now with sudden bursts of speed. Melory and Amorket were long gone, and I hoped the Champion was equal to any mundane difficulties that lay between here and Tsuno. Without them, the stone-things remained agitated, plainly re-membering an intrusion and fumbling out blindly for signs of what had happened. Then one of them latched onto the carcase of its dead kin and began to haul it away.

My people were clustering around me, asking what happened now. I gave the stone-things a few long breaths to see if they were going to become a problem. Their at-titude towards us remained . . . paradoxical. They plainly knew we were there, but they had the animal's awareness of us as *other*, something that smelled or tasted or just *felt* wrong. Not prey, therefore. Nor did they take us as a threat to them, though some animals will run from our very presence and some might attack us if we entered their home like this.

The sensible decision would have been to pull back with what we'd learned. All I felt we'd learned was to ask more questions. That was why I made the decision to press on.

Or, no, it was more than that. What little we had learned told me that these stone-things were not beasts to be driven away, but they remained the business of the Order of Cain. They were outside the realm of the villagers.

I turned to my people, the priest with a congregation again. They were frightened and confused by what we had seen, and I couldn't blame them. I felt the fear in me, too, but blunted by knowledge.

"I've told you of the time the ancestors came to this land," I said, and the old words in this strange place had them frowning and scratching their heads, even Illon, who hadn't heard them so often. "Those of you who've been to the House of our Ancestors have seen the ancestors themselves act it out, how they brought their house across the night sky like a boat. And you all know—better than any villager—that the land they came to was poison to them, so that they sickened, and their children sickened, and they were like to starve and leave nothing but their empty House."

They were nodding along, for all most of them didn't see the connection. The mere familiarity gave them a little strength.

Giving a sermon out here surrounded by the shuffling, questing stone-things was bizarre, but I lifted my voice, using all the tricks I remembered from Sharskin before me, the ways of speaking that put fire and certainty in people's hearts. It's a terrible thing when used for ill, that certainty. I only hoped I was making better use of the priest's mantle than my predecessor.

"Our ancestors came to a compact with this land, and

changed their children so they could eat of the fruit and the meat, and till the land, and in return they would fall prey to the beasts of the wood, and catch the sicknesses of the water, and in all ways be part of the world. But to us is given a gift and a punishment, for the Severance restores us to the Original Condition of our ancestors and places us outside of nature." So much did Sharskin say, but the next words were those Melory and I had added to the creed. "So it is that the Order and the villagers form two halves, they of the world, and we outside it, like day and night, like life and death, the whole stronger than the parts."

I let the echo of my voice ring away, and by then I'd almost forgotten my point, finding comfort myself in the oft-repeated rituals. Then the stone-things knocked against each other, scrabbling close as they, too, tried to understand what had happened, and I remembered.

"The men of the stone-things are no beasts of the wood," I told my followers. "We have seen their bodies, which are like our bodies. We have seen their bones, even, and they are like the bones of a human, not a beast." No mistaking that shattered jaw for the spongy lattice of an animal's skeleton. "And yet the villagers looked on them and knew them to be cast out. They are of the Original Condition like us. That means our ancestors are their ancestors."

"The stone-things ate some of our ancestors?" Graf asked with some disgust.

I had some frayed ends of thought as to what might have happened, but I didn't want to muddy the waters with my speculation. Instead: "We will go deeper into their land now. We will go, because we are the Order, and we do things that the villagers cannot. We will see what secrets we can discover, to turn back the stone-things."

~

We were able to catch up with the corpse-dragger easily enough. Not that it couldn't have hauled the broken bulk of its fellow away swiftly if it had wanted, but the matter seemed to be of no great urgency to it. It stopped and started, seemed to forget what it was doing, then redis- covered the shattered corpse and hauled it another hun- dred yards. It was heading for the huge hill, which was their house and at the same time a gigantic stone-thing.

The thought that, curled up inside it, there might be a great human, some vast, pallid giant, would not quite go away, however many times I banished it.

The lip of the huge shell was tilted up—propped, I thought, by the curve of the land, and yet with purpose, because it allowed the smaller stone-things to creep in and out as though it were a cave. And the aperture they used was plainly the same that, on the smaller scale, would open onto their pale passengers. We trailed the corpse-dragger all the way there and watched it vanish into the dark within, and there our nerve left us for a brief moment. To venture into a dark place full of monsters is bad enough. For that dark place to also be a monster's belly is worse. But beyond all these usual fears was the underlying wrongness of what we'd seen. There was something profoundly unnatural at work that had all of us on a knife-edge.

I reminded myself that we were the lords of the unnatural. We had made ourselves the ambassadors between the people of the villages and that other unseen world the ancestors had come from. The world these stone-men had come from, too. There could be no other way of it. We were cousins beneath the skin, under the shell.

And so I led my people in. It was hard for them to follow me, but I held one secret weapon that would defeat the most mundane of our problems. From my robe I pulled a cracked globe and, with the right passes over its workings, made it give forth light. Not the light of a fire, nor the sun. A strange light that leached the colour from everything it touched, made us seem bleached as the stone-men. A cousin to the lights that glimmered from the walls of the House of our Ancestors, and perhaps to the ghostlight that showed you when a ghost was working through its bearer. The light of another world, brought here across the night sky by those who came before us.

And so, thus fortified, we followed the corpse-dragger into the darkness of the shell.

We were transgressing, venturing into somewhere forbidden. A path we could only walk because we were marked out. Beneath our feet was the flesh of a monster, giving slightly with a rubbery shudder at each footfall. The walls about us were of the same glistening stuff. At first, they were close enough that the stone-thing had to push its way in, but soon they fell away on either side until we were in a high hall like one of the biggest chambers of the House of our Ancestors. Above us, the walls leant in against one another to the seam of a peaked ceiling. Left and right, orifices like gaping toothless mouths quivered, and the stone-things crept in and out on their unguessable errands.

The corpse-dragger hauled its burden through one, and peering after it, we saw three stone-things in a globular chamber, descending on the cadaver. Before we backed off, they had started to dismember it, the human as well as the beast, scouring the broken shell clean of its meat and taking each organ and fragment to the walls. Those walls were already a butcher's collection of pieces and offal. We saw hands, feet, faces all sunk half in, and less recognisable things as well. I could see no reverence for the dead in it. The busy flensing of the stone-things seemed more a frenzy of feeding than mourning.

A second time, my people looked to me to see if this was enough, and perhaps I should have heeded them. Instead, I signalled that we should move deeper into the great shell, past that first hall. So we passed through another gate of the thing's anatomy, and in doing so we stepped from death to new life.

The walls in that larger hall were warty with clear-sided bubbles set into them, each preserving what I thought were more dead specimens at first. Then one twitched, and another, and I realised they lived. More, and likely beyond the intention behind them, they were an education. The smallest of them were little more than shapeless globs of flesh floating in some cloudy medium. Moving along the wall, we found a progression of shape, the coalescing of a hollow skeleton, the growth of spindly limbs. We saw a body that formed like a pair of open hands and then, as it grew, they closed in upon one another, preserving the space between the palms as a chamber within itself. At some point, a button of hard stuff could be seen on the back of those hands, and all the bubbles from there on, larger and larger, showed a growth of shell, built up ridge by ridge. We were watching the growth of the stone-things. The clear blisters on the walls were their eggs, and this room a living hatchery.

My followers wanted to fall on the place with their staves and knives, and perhaps I should have let them. I knew that must prompt a response from our enemies, though, and I was curious and demanded we move on. You may tell stories like this, where a succession of poor choices, three in most cases, leads to the hero learning something better left to ignorance. Melory and I had made the Order into a story, so that the villagers could fit us into their lives, and now I was living one. I was the man in the story you tell, for all you may have told it for generations. I demanded we press on, and you will recall this was the third such time.

At the back end of that chamber, amongst the blisters on the wall, we found something worse. We found the human eggs.

Humans, too, begin as a glob of flesh, but beyond that we are quite different to the stone-things. Watching the stages that turned that formless knot into a recognisable newborn was like seeing a child hollowed out of clay.

We did not see a birth, though the latest sacs held infants that looked as though they should already have come from a mother's womb. In Aro, in any village, you know your Ma. Your Da, most likely not, for who can ever be sure, but the bond between mother and child is often the loss we feel most keenly, when we are cast out.

These children would never wonder where their mother was. She would tower over them, part of the very landscape, visible wherever their shells took them. And that made me wonder how it was: if a stone-thing hatched, was it timed so that a human broke free at the same instant? Or must one wait, forlorn, for the slower sibling to break its membrane and wash out onto the chamber's slick floor? Was there some long apprenticeship, in which the mismatched pair must grow together, or were the two made into one in the moments after that double birth?

"Priest." Graf took my arm, and then Illon said, "I hear a voice."

I had been lost in my own head all this time, and now I came back to myself, because she was right. There was a voice that issued to us from the very bowels of the place. And even I knew, then, that we should have turned back before, but hearing the voice I could not but go see what lips it issued from.

"It speaks . . . I can hear words in it, but not like people say," Illon added, face screwed up as she listened.

I knew the manner of speech, though. I had learned it in the House, for it was how the ancestors spoke. They had a thousand words we did not know, and also they had a particular way of saying even familiar things that made them hard to understand. As though they had built a great tower of language through their long night journey, and it had fallen to ruin after they came here, so that we only had loose beams and sticks of it. This voice, which sounded dry as dead bones, spoke like that.

"And so Jack crept through the giant's castle," said the voice, as we tried to hunt out its origin. We followed the sound of it to one side, ducking under the twitching rim of a doorway and then through a winding length of gut.

"He found many treasures there, while the giant slept. Coins and golden eggs . . ." the voice said, and my followers murmured behind me, wondering what a Jack was.

We came to the ossuary.

That is an Ancestor word. I didn't know it at the time. It means a place of bones.

The walls of that chamber were not just flesh, as everything else. Some process had layered them over with something hard, the same stuff the stone-things' shells were made of, as though to preserve and protect what rested there.

"And he found a talking harp . . ." The crisp, dry voice whispered through the chamber, and I realised that it had grown quieter the closer we came, and that it had been speaking not for its own purposes but to us.

Embedded in the stone wall were bodies, human bodies. There were a half dozen of them, and they were barely more than skeletons covered over with a sparse minimum of flesh. And then over again, with a tissue-thin layer of shell, or else the shell had been them once, and their skin had transformed into it over their long sojourn here.

The attitudes of the bodies in their settings, the frozen expressions on their faces, the way their hands seemed to be clawing out of the stony shell, none of it suggested they had gone to this fate happily.

"And the harp sang most beautifully . . ." Quieter and quieter, leading us past the first couple of petrified dead until we were right in their midst. "So that the giant fell into a great slumber."

I saw the faintest movement, saw the lines of articulation about the stony jaw, the very tongue in the forever-gaping mouth. But I was not ready when the dead man's eyelids clicked up and he stared at me through eyes like grey marbles.

"Hello, Jack," came his parched voice. "I'm Bain."

Interlude

The Sister Colony: Part Four

IT WAS THE RADIO SILENCE that ate Bain alive.

The team back at the ship hadn't sent any more search parties out, no fliers overhead, no land team arduously trekking the many kilometres through the poison forest to reach the coast. Well, he'd expected that. But he had jury-rigged a transmitter now, sending out a steady distress beacon, and nothing. They'd been desperate, he knew. People had been dying since long before the sister team had split away. But surely they could spare a thought for their errant fellows.

And the distress beacon, just pinging into the void, a single voice on a silent planet, singing out to the one ear. Yet that ear was deaf. They weren't listening.

They have forgotten us. The sister colony was nothing more than a footnote in the ship's log. *There went Bain Chan and those doomed souls who followed him into folly.* Still he kept calling into that heedless bandwidth, because what else was there? He just wanted to come home.

Lena hadn't come home. She'd gone hunting snails to provide Geordi with more research material, determined to force the scientific breakthrough they'd come out to make. The third time she'd gone out but not returned. One recovered drone, badly damaged, yielded up a ragged edge of recording, what could only be described as a snail ambush. They had been part-burrowed into the ground. Lena had been intent on more evident prey. That had been it. All of her team had been lost.

There were precisely seven people left in the sister colony now. Abandoning the silent radio, Bain's legs took him meandering about the close confinement of their handful of linked domes. In this one was the cryogenics facility they'd been able to salvage, the embryos they'd taken from the ship so they could make good on the great discoveries they knew they'd make. A hundred tiny frozen dots of life, not enough for a viable colony, but enough for a proof of concept. They'd been going to stride back to the main expedition all full of triumph, declaring their victory over the planet.

And now? Prey for snails.

In another dome he saw Geordi Gownt, still working at his tissue analysis. Bain didn't know if Geordi was remotely on message anymore. The man seemed to be off on some wild tangent of his own, something that simultaneously terrified and fascinated him. Bain had tried to sit through his rambling explanations, but his brain was a soup of stimulants and depressants and sheer fatigue and none of it had gone in.

The rest of their team—*We few, we happy few,* he thought bitterly—were scattered across their tiny domain. Shay Park and someone else were off checking the charged fence they'd put up. Electric shocks had so far deterred the snails, though in a curiously desultory way. As though the creatures could easily break through if they wanted but couldn't be bothered just yet. Other crew were trying to find some biochemical antisnail measure, with the caveat that, for the very reason the things represented such a damned breakthrough, there probably *wasn't* a biochemical antisnail measure. Or not one that wouldn't be fatal to all carbon-based life, humans included.

I just want to sleep. And he had slept, of course. There were surely a few hours of shut-eye in his last four days of activity, except the constant round of ups and downs he was feeding his system had conspired with the slightly off circadian rhythm of the planet to shatter his sense of time. There were parts of his mind that were just flywheeling away all the time, sleep or wake. Others had it worse. Geordi was on record as not having slept at all in twelve days now, as though he was afraid of what he'd dream.

Shay had been talking about leaving, just walking back to the ship. It would be months of journeying. They couldn't possibly transport enough rations, and the whole problem with the planet was that there was nothing they could eat or even safely touch. They were almost out of everything at the base, and yet why just compound that looming problem with the rigours of some arduous cross-country trek?

Bain's feet had taken him back to the radio. Communication had become his obsession, but then since Orindo died and was disassembled and then had partly come back to wave at them, they were short of good technical help. He wondered about going to the lab and putting tools in that slack hand, if it was still animate under Gownt's erratic study. Maybe Orindo was in a position to build a better transmitter than Bain had managed. Left-handed and without a brain. Given the state Bain was in, it still sounded like an improvement.

He stared balefully at the silent receiver, as though he might only now discover he hadn't powered the thing up.

We can't go on like this.

He'd been teetering on the edge of the revelation for a while. Everyone had been waiting for him to make the call, to tell them what to do. *Director, direct.* And so he did what he always did, when his mind reached this far end of its pendulum swing. He called a meeting so that they could demand he did something, and he could sit there knowing there was nothing to be done.

~

Geordi Gownt sat in the corner of the clean room and stared at his specimens. One of them stared back at him. He had given it an eye, just cloned one from his own tissue and dropped it into the thing's cavity wall. He hadn't had to perform anything actually approaching a medical procedure. The snail's tissue had done the hard work automatically. Now it could see him.

He didn't know if it could, of course. And for that matter, how could it? An organ from another world, a different cell structure, the wrong hereditary information, and yet the eye followed him around the room. *Self-portrait of a failing biologist.*

The holographic screens around the room showed him detailed maps of the snail's tissue activity, the complex electrical impulses racing through the entirety of the thing's remaining being. All those parts left over after he'd hacked pieces away for biopsy. It was close to the point where they died, based on his previous subjects. They were robust, but not supernaturally so. Adaptable, though. Both in the sense that they could navigate just about any biochemistry you handed to them, and in the way they could reconfigure the structures of their own bodies, now soft, now hard, now able to exert that murderous strength they'd displayed, even though they'd been limp as jelly the moment before.

He giggled to himself weakly. His latest thought experiment—utterly useless to anyone but then what, precisely, *was* any use anymore—was to imagine if it had been the other way round. What if the snails had built a spaceship, or just adapted themselves to the vacuum somehow. What if *they* had come to *us*? What if it was Geordi Gownt on the table, everted and splayed for study, and some eminent Doctor Snail making learned remarks about the lamentable limitations of Earth biology.

He wondered about making a scale-model spaceship and dropping it in for the cavity lining to explore.

Because it was a remarkable organ, that lining. The very hollow heart of the beast. A sense organ, they'd said, but by now Geordi knew it wasn't just a complex sort of tongue or hand. Whatever went into the cavity triggered a cascade of changes through the snail. It reconfigured its ersatz neurology around what you gave it. *Seeking understanding,* but that wasn't right. That was a human idea.

He reckoned he had it, by now. What went into the snail's inner chamber wasn't just pawed at and inspected, tasted and sniffed. It became a part of the thing's world.

He could almost read the neural changes, now, seeing configurations and structures assembling themselves to represent the new acquisition. Give them a more complex toy, they grew more complex. The one with Orindo Snapper's arm had possessed a remarkable new flourishing of growth. Its horizons had expanded to include human physiology and biochemistry. And, until it disposed of the arm, digested it or spat it out or whatever the process was, the snail's inner world was that much richer.

We have evolved them.

He met his own gaze across the clean room. The splayed, flayed snail seemed to be begging him for release. Or perhaps it was begging him for more. Another eye. A hand. He wondered what would happen if he just lay down there, head on the fleshy thing like a pillow. What would happen if it grew into him and touched his brain. *Oh brave new world that has such people in it!*

The soft chime of a communication snapped him from his morbid reverie. Bain was calling a meeting. Compared to that, the thought of having his brain peaceably devoured by a snail seemed almost merciful, but Geordi levered himself from the floor, made a mumbling apology to the glowering eye, and went to decontaminate.

~

They shambled in, one after another, took their seats at the shoddy little printed table Bain had insisted they spend resources on. Geordi, Shay, all the rest of them. Not Lena. Not Orindo. Not those who had died in the initial attack on the research dome, nor those whose paths had taken them beyond the charged fence and who just hadn't come back. *We're besieged,* Bain told himself. Save that, if you just looked out past the fence, what was there? A badland of salt-saturated soil, the sea one horizon and the trees at another. And rocks, dotted here and there, deceptively random looking. Look long enough and those rocks would move, though. And yet there was no sense of assault, no aggressive charge at the fortifications by an army of snails with catapults and ladders. But anyone going out didn't come back, these days.

"I've called this meeting because . . ." and that was as far as his words took him. *Because. Just because. First lesson of leadership school: always be seen to be doing something. Even when there is nothing to be done.* Haggard eyes stared back at him on every side.

"Because . . ." he repeated, trying to give the word such a determined spin that it would somehow take on a life of its own and come to his rescue.

Geordi Gownt came to his rescue instead. Looking like he'd died a day before, the emaciated biologist raised a hand. "New agenda item, director. I've . . . It's all solved now. I've cracked it. Celebrations are in order." His face was deadpan, his voice level. There was no way to know if this was some misfired joke or if he'd gone mad.

"Perhaps you'd like to elaborate?" At least it got Bain off the hook of having to say the words he didn't have.

"The reason we're here. The incompatibility. The biology of this place." Nice to see all those thousand-yard stares directed at someone else for a change, even though Geordi didn't seem to register them. "I can save us," the xenobiologist said. "We just need... a change of wardrobe. Go... native, you might say."

"What are you—"

"You really should," Geordi shouldered on, and right now his stop-start speech meant it was impossible to know if he'd finished or not, "get hold of the main expedition and tell them."

Bain felt tears spring up in the corners of his eyes. "You know I—"

"Because we can live," said Geordi. "We can... clothe ourselves in this world and... live, director. We have already found the interface that will let us become naturalised here. It's right there." He giggled, a high, horrible sound. "We can live in the snails. But I don't know what it might do to them. We may need to run an impact assessment, director."

"Geordi, I ..." Bain waited, but the expected interruption didn't come. "I don't understand what you're saying. Maybe you should . . ." *Get some rest,* but that went the same for all of them and double for some.

"Maybe I should go put my head in a snail," Geordi said, still utterly without any indication of humour.

A soft chime sounded. Dimly, Bain registered that the perimeter gate had been keyed open. *Home is the sailor, home from the sea, and the hunter home from the hill.* "Geordi," he pressed on, clawing for reason, "can you please put this in some way I can understand?"

"The walls of the snail's internal cavity contain a membrane that acts as a perfect mediator between biologies, any two biologies. I've not . . . I've tried to kill them, poison them, infect them. They'll take anyone, director. Anything."

"But your last report said that you couldn't isolate the effect. You said it was"—Bain raked through his crumbling memory—"distributed throughout the organism. It's not like we can just skin them and wear them,"

Again that ghastly titter. "*We* can't wear *them,* no," Geordi said sepulchrally. "But—"

"Who just came in?" Shay asked suddenly. "That was the gate. Who just came in? We're all here."

Bain felt that he should feel some dreadful shock, but he just sat there. It was easier to just sit there. Across the table, Geordi trembled, blinking rapidly.

They all heard the chime of the airlock being accessed. In the chasm of everyone else's silence, Geordi's giggle was appallingly loud.

"I worked it out," he said, a reverent whisper as though to make up for it. "We're saved," meeting Bain's eyes with his bloodshot orbs.

They heard the shriek of abused metal, the whip of plastics suddenly released as the first snail forced its way in. *But they could have just come through the walls,* Bain thought numbly. *Why did they bother to knock?* Everyone else was on their feet, shouting, screaming. He just sat there, scrolling down the virtual agenda as though *snail attack* was somewhere there close to *any other business.* Geordi met his gaze again and mouthed the word *saved.*

They forced their way into the central dome, their ridged shells stretching the fabric to tearing point and beyond, their hideous grey arms scrabbling at the edge of the doorway like gigantic fingers. Shay attacked the first one, and it flicked her away irritably, still trying to negotiate the ruin of rods and rips it had made. A second monster came in half over the top of it, clambering across the shell and then descending onto the part-collapsed dome roof, shearing through it to crash onto the table, scattering everyone. Bain just sat there, still somehow in his chair, although the rest of his precious meeting had been strewn to the winds. The snail reared up before him, standing high so that its finger-fringed mouth gaped, so that he could see within to the hollow heart of it.

Lena Dal looked back. Lena Dal reached for him, arms part melded to the oozing substance of the snail's interior. Scattered fragments of Geordi's words rattled about in his head. *They beat us to it,* he thought. *We were going to wear them, but they beat us to it.*

Lena Dal's face twisted, something trying to express itself through her. At the same time, it was her face, and she was still behind it. She said his name.

It wasn't the radio silence that ate Bain alive.

IX

I WAS PROUD OF my people, then. Faced with this prodigy, if any had run, all would have run. I would have run. The Bandage-Men live on the edge of natural and unnatural, but this was so far into the latter that we were lost in its wilds.

The crisp voice said something else, but the weird, antique inflection meant I didn't catch the words to translate them. *Click-click* went those hard eyelids over the pearls of the man's eyes.

I said that if any had run, I would have. In truth, had they not been there, I'd have been gone from that chamber in a heartbeat. It was the Order at my back that kept me there, because I was priest and they relied on me. Sometimes strength is a strange thing, owned by none and yet everyone borrows it from their neighbour.

"My name is Handry," I said, "of the Order of Cain."

The thing that called itself Bain gave a small, rattling sound that wasn't really a laugh. "And are you marked so that, though all men's hands be turned against you, yet they are not permitted to slay you?"

I almost collapsed then, legs gone to water. Then I remembered where Sharskin had gotten his talk of Cain and marks. It was a story of the ancestors, one of their library of mostly incomprehensible doggerel that had taken his fancy.

"Bain," I addressed it. "What are you?" I tried to say it as the ancestors would.

"A talking harp owned by a giant. Or, if you are Cain, let me be Jonah who has sung to Leviathan and lulled him to sleep, for now, so that I may speak with you. And yet I am nothing. I am the snail who dreams it is a philosopher, and thinks itself a philosopher dreaming of the snail." And other nonsense I cannot now recall. Its jaw hinged and the segmented tongue flexed, but they were like a child's toys for which the child provides the voice. Bain spoke to me like the ancestors in the House do, the sound originating invisibly within it.

"You came here across the night sky."

"Across . . ." Its voice trailed off, and for three breaths it was just a dead thing, all animation gone from it. Then the stone eyes rolled, and it said, "Yes. The night sky. To make a new home in this land." Only it used the ancestors' word, which meant a land hanging like a ball in the night, not just a far place one might walk to. "And what are you, Handry of Cain? For I have not smelled the blood of a true human for a long time. The beasts of this land are not like us, Handry. Though I will tell you a secret. There are beasts in this land that walk like us, have bodies like us, even speak with words that are like ours, but they are not humans. The poison of this land courses through their veins. I am a scientist, Handry, and when I am conjured by Leviathan, I try to solve this mystery, but I cannot."

It was a strange thing, to stand before something as ancient and uncanny as Bain, and know I understood the world better than it did. It must mean the people of Portruno, or some other place the stone-things had encountered. They had shown me and mine a peculiar deference, recognising the Original Condition in us. For those others, no such mercy had been extended. In finding a balance with the nature of this land, they had made themselves no more than beasts in the eyes of Bain.

"If you are human," I said, following its own usage carefully, "how are you not poisoned?" Even then, in our extremity, the thought came to me that this was something Melory or Iblis could find a use for. I realised I was standing taller, the embodiment of the Order, staff planted in the rubbery floor, the standard my people rallied around.

Bain made the nonlaughing sound again, as though ossified parts of it had come loose within its rib cage. "We sought to tame Leviathan," it told me, "for in the stomach of the monster we found the secret of life. And yet, when we came to it and set our strength against his, it was Leviathan who triumphed, and tamed us. And at first, I was joined with one of the Children, and we became more than we had been. And then, when that Child ailed, they brought me here to Leviathan so that I might dwell forever within her thoughts. And now I am no more than the dream of Leviathan."

"You are all the dreams of Leviathan," another voice came. Only because it issued from a different dead mouth did I know it for a separate speaker.

"Quiet, Geordi," Bain hissed, but the new tones croaked on.

"There is nothing of us but Leviathan and her dreams," uttered the thing called Geordi. "I told you. Before she took us, I told you. Whatever she swallows becomes her mind. Whatever she takes within herself becomes a dream in her, and though she is slumberous and insensate, those dreams can think for her and advise her and give her a mind and a purpose. And so she calls to the Children, our Children, in the voice we give her, and they act as her hands and haul her across the land. You stand within her, and so you will be her dreams soon enough, and perhaps you will guide her purpose when she dreams you."

I took all my borrowed courage and leant in close to

Bain, staring, trying to see the life in the petrified corpse. "Dreams," I echoed.

Rattle. Click. Geordi droned on. "Whatever is placed upon Leviathan's altar becomes real in her imagination. She conceives only of those things that the Children give her, just as their worlds consist only of those things that they devour and hold within themselves. What a thing we made, when we wrestled Leviathan and let her swallow us."

"A great thing." A third voice, that was the same voice. Another ancient corpse spoken for. "A purpose. Survival. For we were beset by the world and betrayed by our kin, and we would have died. Now we live forever in the dreams of Leviathan."

"Lena, I am director. I speak for us," Bain interrupted peevishly, but the one called Lena ignored him.

"We are the masters of this land," she said. "Better become a dream of Leviathan than let our Children devolve into beasts." And there was a hard tone to the old voice that reminded me of another man, who'd spoken of destinies and purposes and a grand crusade against those who lived as part of the world.

"Your Children you speak of, they are the human children or the stone-things? The shell-bearers who carry them. Your people ride them, or . . . ?"

"A symbiosis of alien and human," said the voice coming

from Geordi. "Unintentional, unanticipated. Unprecedented. In investigating and absorbing us, replicating our complexity within itself, the native fauna becomes a mirror that shows us our likeness. And though we perish, the reflection lives on so long as our bones remain interred here."

Ghosts, I thought. That was what they had become. But unlike the expert system ghost in Melory's head, or even the voices of the House, these truly were the ancestors speaking to me.

"It wasn't worth it," Bain said, surprising me, but then Lena came back with, "It was!" As forceful as that withered voice could be. "We survive. We preserve the colony. We are all that is left."

I took a deep breath, steadying myself. "You say the beasts they brought you looked human. You must know that those are also your Children, born of the same ancestors." A hard thing to phrase when you speak to the very ancestors themselves, people who in their own flesh had seen the night sky from within, had known the House when it still moved.

They all spoke, and I had to concentrate to disentangle them. Bain was saying, "No, they are but beasts," and Geordi, "We had no proof from the expedition that their experiments had born fruit," but Lena told the truth behind the other two lies. "If that is so," she said, "then they are our rightful prey, for they abandoned us and our Children in the wilderness. We are owed our revenge against them."

"But not you," Bain said, in the tangled echo of all that. "You seem as our Children to us. Or as the children of our parents. Have you come from our far home?"

I almost said yes. I had wild thoughts of making a compact with the voices, bargaining so that they turned away from the places where people dwelled. That seemed an eminently fitting thing for a priest to accomplish. But then Geordi added, "You must sit with us. We are hungry to understand all that you have learned. Let us have all your dreams of our home." And I had a sudden thought about just what a long conversation with these ghosts might mean. I had no wish for a stone prison, nor eternal life as a dream of this Leviathan.

I took one step back. I had worked out by then that, just as the stone lips made no words, the stone eyes saw nothing, no more than an echo of a remembered sense. And yet, as we started to pad back the way we had come, Bain called out.

"You must not leave," it said, almost plaintively. "We have such things we can learn from you. New things. It has been so long since anything new came to us." And, as we were crowding the entrance, about to sally to the egg chamber, "It is lonely, being a dream. It is hard, being a fossil in the mind of a giant. We cannot change by ourselves. We cannot become new things. We rehearse the same arguments, over and over. We are frozen in time at the moment Leviathan took hold of us. Do not go, Handry of Cain. Bring your stories to us so that we can become something new." An old, old man calling from his deathbed for someone to comfort him. And, despite everything, I felt a pang of pity in my heart.

But not enough to turn back, and so we pushed out to where the blisters hung over us, with their developing burdens. I thought again about trying to destroy as many as we could then, a mass infanticide to slow down the stone-things in their expansion. But I don't know if it would have achieved anything, and I am sure it would have called down the wrath of Leviathan on us. Two of her Children were even then tending the brood. We hurried on past them.

From behind us, the voice of Bain lifted, edged with anger. "The singing harp cried out," it called, "'Master, here are thieves come to steal your treasures!' And the giant broke from his slumber and bellowed, 'I smell the blood!'"

A convulsion seemed to ripple through the walls around us, not strong but vast. Leviathan stirred. The stone-things there paused in their work, as though hearing a voice we could not, the same voice the ghosts used to speak to one another.

"Go!" I drove my followers before me, out into that first chamber, where the tilted rim of the shell and the edges of its mouth gave us a sight of the outside air. Before we had run halfway, though, a shadow fell across the exit. One of the larger stone-things shunted its way into the gap and stayed there, so that there was barely a hand's span of space above it, and none on either side.

"What will you do now, Jack?" called the voice of Bain from the depths of Leviathan. "I have rolled a stone before my home. Or are you Odysseus as well? I will devour you, Jack, and you will join me in the dream."

"We can upend it," one of my people said, but I could see how the creature had latched onto the floor and the edges of the gap, made itself no more than the newest and hardest section of the enclosing walls.

"Back and destroy the eggs," said Graf, but there were more stone-things behind us now, not rushing at us with that furious speed but advancing nonetheless. I felt they still felt our Severance, because it was akin to something within them. Their passengers, or hosts, or parasites, the things within them whose human thoughts had become their animal dreams, they knew the Mark of Cain upon us.

"The walls themselves," Illon said. She had a knife out, a Jasp-wood blade, not even the metal of the House. "They are flesh. We can cut them." And that seemed the least worst of all our bad options.

Even as we veered away towards the closest expanse of clammy, oozing wall, though, something struck my head. In the shocked instant of contact I thought it was a sling-stone. My mind instantly pictured a shell tilted up, its pale occupant pushing its way out into the air, whipping a missile at me. In the next moment I realised shock was all I'd suffered, and the missile was rising up into the cavernous space. I tracked it, trying to understand what I was seeing.

From outside there came a great commotion. I heard a handful of human voices lifted in desperate war cries, but behind that, a thundering chorus of *Brack! Brack!*

Rescue! And yet we were in the very heart of the stone-thing's domain, in the bowels of their Leviathan that dreamed it was a convocation of the ancestors whose whims it pursued. Then the thing that had struck my head was back, arcing past me and joined by its siblings.

A wasp. More than that, a Fury. I saw them deter-minedly swarming in over the top of the blockading stone-thing, spinning about in the air and making abortive sallies against us. I shouted at them to attack the walls, but they would never pay any heed to me. Most of them seemed to be on the verge of making me their target.

Bain was shouting again, that dead voice surely rattling

every petrified bone of his corpse. He was shouting in panic, though. "Where are the Children?" he demanded. "What have you done? We are *blind*!"

The stone-thing in the doorway had lost its hold, retreating partway and lifting its shell up so that the buttons of its eyes waved at us. So that the gaping maw at its centre opened and a timorous human face emerged, hands prying at the slick edge. I saw utter terror on that face. Human terror.

Melory had used Amorket's wasps to cloak us before, of course, when we killed one of them. Now she had come back for us, and at the head of an army.

By then, half my people were already chasing ahead of any orders I might give them. We charged the stone-thing, and I saw an expression of horror and despair on its human face before that visage was retracted into its innards like a tongue.

It took every one of us, but we upended the thing and rolled it aside, bursting out into a chaos of fighting. The brackers had driven into the stone-things' camp in a great wedge, smashing down with their armoured forelegs, trying to shatter every shell they could reach. Their enemies were fighting furiously, swarming them from many sides, attacking where they could catch the brackers unprepared, hunkering down when the reprisal came. At the edge of the valley wall, I saw a handful of humans. It was

Erma and her hunters mostly, whipping slingstones at the stone-things, trying to keep them down with spears when the beasts scrabbled for them. Melory was there, too, and Amorket stood empty-handed below, jostled by the brackers. She had her arms outstretched as though inviting her death, and the tide was turning even as we raced through the melee, so that death was surely coming for her. I saw her mark me, and then I cannoned into her, taking her by the waist and hauling her back up the side of the valley. I felt three fierce stings from the Furies for my trouble, but without poison. I hope that meant she understood I was trying to save her.

By then the brackers were reconsidering their assault, or else this lightning strike had been the whole of their plan. They had broken open a full dozen of the stone-things, and the sight was hideous, the pinkish pulp of their unshelled bodies half disgorging human forms that tried to crawl away or writhed like gugworms exposed to the sun. Some got clear and flailed and slithered towards the sheltering bulk of Leviathan. Others were still merged with the beast that had carried them, by the hair, by the limbs, by the head. The brackers killed them when they could, and yet there were many of their own left broken in the mud by that point. The stone-things were stronger than they.

A new wave of bustling shells was sweeping along the

valley, formed up into a monstrous wall, and that was all the encouragement everyone needed to quit the field. The first battle in our war with the stone-things ended in a hurried retreat that the Furies covered, confounding the enemy when they tried their soundless speech one to another until we humans reached Tsuno and the brackers their own place within the village's land.

I knew it would not be long before the stone-things regrouped and came to exact their vengeance.

X

BY THE TIME WE were away from the stone-things, the fever had come over me. Where Amorket's Furies had lanced me, my body swelled up, red and angry. Not poison—I have no doubt those wasps possessed a venom that would have killed me outright. When we of the Original Condition are injured, though, this is the risk we always run. Like Kalloi, I was fighting the hysterical reaction of my own flesh to the intrusion of the outside world.

Once again, my personal history saved me. They never did quite Sever me, back in Aro. So it was that the sufferings of the outcast were always a little blunted. I was two days out of my mind as I thrashed and dreamed and sweated, but for half of that I was recovering. Amorket's directive from the hive of Jalaino would not be fulfilled just then.

Many things happened in those two days.

For one, my Bandage-Men wanted to kill Amorket, and came very close to simply bludgeoning and knifing her, wasps or no wasps. They saw the marks of stings on my flesh and read into them an intent I don't think she possessed. Melory stood between them and their revenge, and only their respect for her, as the sage who interpreted the voices of the ancestors, stayed their hands.

For another, I dreamt of terrible things. Between the fever and what we had seen within Leviathan, I can be forgiven, I think. In my nightmarish thrashings, I was back in those living halls, back before the stone speaker of the stone-things that called itself Bain and Lena and Geordi. I was sinking into the flesh of that giving floor, into the slick walls. I was being dragged into the gulfs of the beasts by pallid, nail-less hands. I was locked in a withered fossil of a body, trapped forever in that dry company, speaking riddles and nonsense in the crooked language of the ancestors. In two brief days of fever, I lived a hundred years of horror. But when the fever broke, I was left with a dreadful revelation: that I had a weapon against Leviathan and her brood, and that my nightmares might yet be a true revelation of what was to come.

The other major change in circumstances was evident to me when I came back to myself and opened my eyes, for we were not in Tsuno, nor any village. We were out under the stars, under makeshift shelters, amongst the trees. My followers were there, and Melory and Amorket. In fact, my first sight on waking was both Illon and the

Champion of Jalaino at my sickbed, the former glowering at the latter and the latter looking . . . stricken. Grieving. Amorket, my nemesis, grieving because she thought she might have slain me. I was looking at her thin, sharp face when she realised I was awake, and I cannot quite explain the expression on it. Oh, guilt, certainly, and a residue of the old hate and anger that was never specifically for me or the Order, but just for her predicament and that of her village. But there was a need there: a need for me not to be dead. We were comrades, she and I. And she was cut off from the people of the villages in her own way, and had found a place amongst us, in her own way. For a queasy moment I saw she and I bound together as the stone-things and their human passengers, but that passed, and I found I was glad of her. An arm's length gladness, given the ache of the stings, but there isn't much gladness in the story of the Bandage-Men. You take what you can get.

Beyond the lean-to they had me in, I saw far more, stretching off between the trees. Not just Erma's hunters, but the whole of Tsuno's people, young and old. They had evacuated the village entirely, moving at an angle away from the stone-things. Melory would tell me the thought behind what had been her plan. The enemy was coming, and we had seen what they had done to Portruno. The hope was they would follow the people and not pause to destroy Tsuno's tree. She had planned for that eventuality as well, though, using her ghost to coax wasps down from the hive, which might serve as seed for a new colony should the village be destroyed. Melory had been very busy over those two days, in between saving me and saving Tsuno. She had been in constant communion with the House, across all the miles of forest, drawing on its thoughts and ideas. I was not the only one with a plan.

As well as the Tsuno folk, Erma's scouts had found a contingent of refugees from Portruno, lost in the forest, hungry and ailing, and brought them with us. Many of their kin had been killed when the stone-things stormed their village. Many more had died in the woods, to beasts, to hunger, to mischance or eating the wrong thing. When they learned that their very tree was gone, most of the rest looked as though they would rather have gone the same way. Tsuno's young Lawgiver, I'm told, gave a fine speech, welcoming them, promising them homes and a place in the world. When I saw him myself, he seemed a taller man, a stronger one. He was lawgiver in truth as well as merely the bearer of the ghost.

What I also saw, out under the trees, were the brackers. They had their own camp and had already made some of their odd little treehouses there. It was right up against the camp of the villagers, both sides acting as though an unseen wall lay in between. Erma and her hunters were the only ones to cross, and I saw then with their red standards and their whistles, bringing gifts to the brackers and back to their own people. Their secret was out, then, and I saw how it had changed them in the eyes of the Tsuno folk. I would talk with Erma, soon after. I would be open with her about the Bandage-Men, how the Order interacted with the villages, how we maintained our knife-edge existence. She was not Severed, but she had a touch of our condition now. If her mystery continues to later generations, I suspect it will do so clad in a bracker-mask, in bestial pantomime, with pipes and flags for human eyes to match those they use for the animals. And we will help her, if we can. The Order needs all the allies it can get.

But we would first have to survive the stone-things, for they were coming to seek their own vengeance for their dead, or perhaps they were seeking more food for the dreams of Leviathan. Whichever it was, they were coming.

~

When I was strong enough to sit up, Melory and I spoke long into the night about what I'd learned. She'd heard it all from my people already, and by the time I opened my mouth, she had a far better understanding of Bain and the stone-people than I did, taught by the piecemeal lessons of the ancestors. We did not know just what had gone on that had led to the stone-things and their inhabitants, but we knew that in those days, the ancestors had been desperate for any way to live in this land.

I cannot imagine anyone being that desperate, but I was not there. I cannot judge them.

"So, it's run and run from them," I said, at that fire. "And in the end every village will have to run, and every tree will be torn up by the roots, and that will be the end no matter how good we are at running. Or it's fight."

Melory nodded, eyes full of thinking.

"I have a plan," I told her.

"I have one, too."

We exchanged plans, she and I. She didn't like mine, which was fine because neither did I. We both preferred hers, but mine seemed more likely to work, both because hers required the cooperation of Amorket, and because she was not sure if she could *reprogram* Amorket's Furies in the way she wanted. Getting it wrong might do nothing, or it might make things so very much worse. *Reprogram* was the ancestors' word for it. She could not turn the Furies from their chief purpose, which was hate and fear of the Order. She could place a leash on that purpose, she hoped.

Hope was most of the little we had. The remainder, which was to say, my plan, was despair.

"Are you strong enough to march?" she asked me. The stone-things were moving faster than we were, and our lead had been devoured. When I'd looked out across the displaced villagers, everyone of an age to bear a staff or a sling was armed. They were going to turn back with the dawn and try to drive off the enemy, or at least slow them. The chance to actually triumph lay only with us. Even with the brackers on our side, we had seen the stone-things were stronger.

When I was speaking to Erma, I asked how she had led the brackers to our rescue. She had not, she said. The assault had been their own idea, for they hated the stone-things for driving them from their own village. She had simply latched on and brought Melory and Amorket with her, in the hope that they could be of some aid. The brackers would fight when we fought, she said, and she could communicate our intent to fight to them, but they had lost many and would not be leading the charge. She was upset, saying this. I realised that, to her, they were not just beasts, nor even just *the brackers*, but individuals she knew from their markings and adornments. They were people, to her.

In truth, I did not feel strong enough to march, and Melory must have known, doctor as she was. But the stone-things would not give me time to regain my strength. If the Bandage-Men were to fulfil our role, in the story we told about ourselves, we would have to go and fight for Tsuno and all the villages that next dawn, and I would have to go with them.

~

The next morning, feeling sick and with every joint aching, I beheld Leviathan.

When they told me the stone-things were chasing at the heels of the Tsuno folk, I had pictured the beasts themselves. I knew they could be swift, and imagined them striding on their long legs between the trees, the sharp edges of their shells scarring the trunks as all the beasts of the wood fled before them.

That was all true, and just as I foresaw, save that in their wake, Leviathan walked. She came on her own legs, that were thicker around than the trunks of the trees, than any house built by human hands. The trailing edge of her tilted shell left a furrow in the earth half as wide as a village as limbs clawed her forwards, clutching at the ground and digging in like human fingers. She came at the speed of a human in a hurry, not quite a run but not idling. She was vast as the House of our Ancestors, and I wondered if the sight of that colossus in motion had been as awe-inspiring.

I imagined the brittle voice of Bain within her, driving her on just as I was telling myself even then that I must go on. We all have a council of voices in our minds to prod us forwards or pull us back, but with Leviathan those voices had once been men and women, ancestors who had been devoured, or else entered into a compact with her to save themselves from the killing land.

There seemed to be little awareness amongst the stone-things that our forces were drawn up against them. They did not slow for us. Rather than let them crash into us with all their momentum, we hastily called out the order to advance, and in fits and starts all the fighting people of Tsuno and Portruno, everyone strong enough to wield a club or throw a stone, rushed forwards. When the brackers saw what we were about they followed, and quickly overtook us on the left. They would fight to their own plan, though, and retreat on their own recognisance. Erma could not speak enough to them to make them part of our scheme. And yet they knew us as allies against a far greater threat.

We did not try the stone-things strength against strength. That would have been fatal. Instead the village folk engaged and fell back, swirled around the sides of the individual stone-things, flung stones, made speed and chaos their allies. And there was much shouting and

whooping, battle-chants and old songs and simple in-
sults. What harm it did the enemy, I don't know, but it
did us good to vent our fury at them. And in the midst of
all of it, my Order was the head of the spear we thrust towards Leviathan.

Between our nature and Melory's soundless shouting,
the stone-things were still slow to strike at us, and some
even lurched out of our way unbidden. Like the more
cunning beasts, though, they could reach past what they
felt for us. Mathoc was crushed, and perhaps that was
just a blundering misstep, but then Barial fell, and Tan-
nari, and I knew that the stone-things were battering at
the forbiddance to get to us, fighting against their own
senses and natures. I saw the stone hand of Bain in those
deaths. Leviathan dreamt human dreams, and through
them knew that we were a threat.

In the centre of our formation ran Amorket and I.
Not Melory: she remained behind the fighters because
I would not risk her. She had none of my protections,
and the Order would survive my loss far better than it
would survive hers. The two of us, though, we were to
be the point of the knife when we struck against the
stone-things, me for my plan, Amorket for Melory's. And
around us, the sheath of that knife was being worn away
by too much use. Some of my followers died; others were
just separated from us, or ran left or right to lead some

marauding stone-thing away and could not rejoin our ranks. And with every step I grew weaker.

Leviathan loomed ahead through the trees, already impossibly large, and still clutching her way towards us. Yet we had forgotten how vast she was. Though we sought to reach her, and she tried to close that same gap, still we were far from her. Amorket's wasps danced round us in a frenzy of frustration and in their buzz, I heard Melory's voice.

I had to reach Leviathan. I had to cast myself into her very jaws. That was my plan, and now you see how wretched a plan it was. I would give myself to her dreams just as Bain had wanted. I would make myself a thorn in her conscience. I would *change her mind* by becoming a part of it. In those unreal spaces, I would do battle with Bain and the others and turn aside Leviathan. And be her prisoner, forever and forever, as the stone grew over my wasting form.

I told you Melory's plan was better.

I fell to my knees abruptly, there in the very heart of the battlefield. Illon hauled me up and I managed another few steps, but abruptly my breath would not come, and I doubled forwards and tried to vomit out the nothing in my stomach. My people formed a perimeter about me, but there were fewer and fewer, the stone-things jostling and grinding on all sides. Illon was shouting at me, and I was trying to shout at myself, all the voices in my head united in telling me I *must* get up.

I got up, and then a stone-thing sheared through our group, knocking me over, scattering my people, crushing Graf, then wallowing off as though panicked. Before we could regroup, there were others filling the space it had made. They were not attacking us, exactly. We would have been dead in instants if they were. They were trying to find us, though, trying to bridge that gap in their minds that would turn us into enemies they could act against. I saw their shells tilt up, maws gaping, human faces blinking anxiously out to see what and where we were.

A hand had one of my arms, a hand had the other. I was being jolted forwards, my legs trying to get numb feet beneath me to carry my weight. Illon had me; Amorket had me. Jalaino's Champion met my gaze, her face taut with desperation; with joy. Amorket was trying to haul me to my death. Perhaps that satisfied her Furies. Amorket was trying to achieve her own death. Perhaps that, too, would suffice. Or she was trying to get herself close enough to Leviathan to give Melory's plan a chance. Or all these things.

We were past more stone-things. Leviathan filled all the world before us. My legs would not take my weight. I was like a dead thing myself, to be cast as an offering to appease the monster. And that, too, seemed fitting for the legend the Order had made about itself. Then a great shelled beast rushed into us and one of its legs lashed out and kicked Amorket in the chest and flung her aside.

Illon shrieked and opened a long line across its flesh, and it recoiled, more from her than the knife. I found I could run after all, stumbling across the broken ground until I collapsed by Amorket, my moment of strength gone.

Her fingers dug into my arms as she sat up. Her face was such an old friend to pain that I didn't realise her leg was broken until I saw the crooked way it lay beneath her.

Illon was with us a moment later, seeing all. She was shouting, but the blood was so loud in my ears I couldn't hear her. A moment later she began striking Amorket, beating her fists against the knotted wood of the Champion's armour, shaking her, screaming in her face, even swatting at the Furies as they came to investigate.

Amorket stared at her, and because I was looking into her face, I saw the moment she relaxed. I saw the *yes* she had been denying herself since before she ever came to Orovo. She let the Furies off their leash and set them on Illon.

And yet she must have held the very trailing edge of that leash, somehow. Or else it was Melory's *reprogramming,* for Illon got up and sprinted towards Leviathan's leading edge, that canted shell, that hungry mouth that could have swallowed the house I was born in. The Furies seethed in confusion, an angry cloud above me, before chasing her. They gave her time.

You have heard stories where the youngest brother is the bravest one, the youngest sister the cleverest. We all have. Those junior siblings, who dare things their elders do not, who triumph against all odds and then return with bounty to their people.

They are half-true, those stories.

She vanished into the maw of Leviathan, and the Furies swarmed in after her, and none of them emerged again.

Then the Order had caught up with us and were dragging me away. The villagers were in full retreat, the brackers also. We must flee or be abandoned and overwhelmed. They took me, despite anything I might have said. Because I was clutching her to me and would not let go, they took Amorket also.

XI

THE NEXT DAY, I had my strength again. Or enough of it to go see how things were, between us and the stone-things.

Many of the Tsuno folk had died, and of Portruno, and of the brackers. But *many* meant that most were still alive, from all three forces. They had been fighting to give us time for our own mad plans, after all. Or the humans had, and brackers had struck, broken shells and then fallen back according to their own schemes, and so preserved as many of theirs as they could.

Overnight, the stone-things had not overhauled our camp, and that gave Melory hope that some part of her plan had succeeded, and what she had taught the Furies had become part of Leviathan's dream.

I went without Amorket, who was one of many patients Melory and Tsuno's doctor were tending to. I went with a couple of the Order who I'd told to abandon me and run if things went bad. But I went with hope and with my staff of office, and between their twin supports, I reached the battlefield.

The stone-things were still there, forming their own camp of shells about Leviathan. I told my helpers to wait and went forth alone to meet them.

They stirred uneasily as I came, those heavy shells. I saw them tilt and angle, and eyes glinted at me from beneath hoods of flesh and stone. I thought I heard the weak whisper of their human voices, one to another.

I set my staff in the earth and they drew back from me, the edges of their shells scraping together.

I took one more step, though I felt as if I should collapse there and then. Leviathan herself stirred and fell back before me. In her body were all the Furies that Amorket had hatched from her flesh, that bore the poison of Jalaino—not a venom for the flesh but one for the mind. If Melory had failed in her preparations, then perhaps the stone-things would have inherited only hate for us, and I would have been destroyed, and they would have followed the Order to the ends of the world in their need to obliterate us. And in that way, we might still, perhaps, have saved the villages. But Melory had spoken long hours with Amorket, and she understood the heart of Jalaino. Melory knew that village's drive to fight us was rooted only in fear, which fear now lived in the dreams of Leviathan. We had become the monsters the stone-things warned their Children about.

I held my staff up at the heights of Leviathan and she

cowered, as a mountain might cower. She shuffled away from me. She picked up her shell and fled, in her ponderous manner, and the stone-things crowded in her churned wake and followed.

~

An epilogue, of sorts.

A hundred days later, as the Tsuno folk say, meaning just... later, after the memories of the war with the stone-things had been given a chance to dull. I am standing at the outskirts of Jalaino. We are due a reckoning. My heart is very heavy.

My people stand farther out, at the tree line, because this is my moment, and this is my risk to take.

I can see Amorket, limping from the last of the houses, out into the fields where I'm waiting for her. Her tread seems heavy as my heart. Things have sat many different ways between us now, since she first confronted me in Orovo, but she is looking forward to this no more than I.

Behind her, the people of Jalaino are gathered to watch. Among them are the other Champions, far too many of them, each tired and sick and bent under the weight of their ghosts. Each with the hives that feed on them even as they feed them, their wasps busying the air.

She stops when she is still twenty paces from me, and

her new Furies rise from within the twisted wooden armour. I hate the sound of them. They make me fear them, as though they were placing ghosts in my mind.

"I am Handry of the Order of Cain!" I call out, loud enough that they can all hear me. "We have made our camp at the edge of your village! If you have beasts, we shall drive them away! If you have word, we shall bear it! If you have outcasts, we shall claim them as our due! Now, what words have you for us?"

I see her gather herself. "Only this, that you have outstayed your welcome! Begone!" Though I say so myself, she is not the speaker I am. Her voice is scratchy and thin, more a screech than anything else. Still, they hear her.

"What if we will not?" I demand of her, of them all. "We have come to your door. We see your fires and your feasts and all the good things you have! What if we demand them?" And the people of Jalaino pull together, because this is their fear. This is what the tree learned from them, that it gave forth the Champions to defend them.

"Then I drive you out!" Amorket shrieks, her voice breaking on the last word, and her Furies rush forth to swarm me, thickening the air, battering at me. I lift my arms, covering my face. I brace against the stings, even as I draw my robe about me and flee, a pitiful figure; a shadow gone back to the dark between trees. A nightmare woken from. I make myself a comic thing, yelling, cursing, diminishing; a thing they have power over. A thing not to be feared.

It is as simple as that. Mostly because Melory has gone to Jalaino and spoken with the hive and the ghosts and done what she can to reprogram them. But this was their fear, and this was the need the Champions arose to satisfy. They wished to be safe from us, and now they have seen that they have power over us. They always had power over us, of course. We outcasts were only ever their victims, but they were too scared of us to realise it.

I turn back, at the trees' edge. Amorket stands, lopsided, slump-shouldered. Behind her, the crowd of villagers has changed, relaxed. The ghost that was their fear is no longer shining out of their faces.

~

How will things go with the stone-things? We have met them three times now, once again near Tsuno, twice elsewhere but in the same quarter. Each time one of the Order has stood before them, defied them, denied their ravening claim to the land, and they have fled before us. The bans that Melory placed within them through Amorket's wasps have held. Problem solved, you would think, except life is not that simple.

We must do something about the stone-things, by

which I do not mean simply drive them away. They are the descendants of the ancestors, too. I remember those pale, toothless faces as they squinted out at us from their living houses that were also their prisons. I remember Bain's grief when it could not feel the presence of its Children. They are not merely dreams of Leviathan, but humans who have grown up in a strange village, with strange customs and strange ghosts guiding them. If we can make a compact with the brackers, we can find a way to compact with them, too. Because they are our estranged siblings, and if anyone should have sympathy with the estranged, it is we of the Order.

~

I return to our camp, off in the woods, and we eat ship-food, and something that Iblis has let Melory grow in some of the fields Orovo no longer needs, from when it was bigger. It is something like the phenna we had in Aro, which you can cook or stew or grind for flour. It is sickly looking and tastes bad, and yet it feeds us, a little. We cannot live off it forever, but we can at least use it to supplement the food of the ancestors. Melory is still working on the problem, but these days she is talking about making ghosts, too. She wants a new ghost that we can carry with us, because there is only one of her. A Melory ghost, because what we saw within Leviathan showed us that such things can be done.

That night, Amorket shuffles out to our fire and sits with me. Her armour is gone, and I can see all the angry pits and burrows on her bare shoulders and arms.

"It worked," she confirms. "The tree feels . . . safe now. The wasps . . . have stopped biting." And Melory thinks the wasps will return once we do, that we can perform our song and dance at Jalaino, and after a day or so the tree will feel a build-up of our presence, and grow sick of us, and reawaken the Champion ghosts, just as a day or so of some berry or grain will make us outcasts grow sick from eating it. It will have a *reaction* to us, Melory says, and then Amorket or some other will come and we will speak the same sort of words, and she will drive us away. We have added to our rituals and our legends. Sooner or later, even those villagers with no Champions will have some villager chosen to don the ritual wooden armour they'll make and drive us off when we have performed our chores and taken our due. And they will feel safer. And we will *be* safer, that much more entrenched in their world as the villains they can offload their evil onto and then drive out.

Amorket leans into me and grips my hand. Words hang between us, not the ritual exchange but the real words we could not say there, and do not say now. *I wish you didn't have to go. I wish you could come with us. I wish . . .*

We went through a lot together, at Tsuno. I hated and feared her, and she bore a whole village's hate and fear of me. But in the end, it was the two of us and Illon against the world, and Illon died. And I am a man who once imagined what it might be, to be with a woman, and unless and until Melory makes some breakthrough, I must never become close to any woman who bears the Mark of Cain. Nor would any woman of the villages tolerate my wooing. Save Amorket, who knows what it is like to be marked out.

And now she returns to her people. And now I must depart with mine.

"We will come back this way," I tell her. *In a hundred days, as the Tsuno folk say.*

"I will be waiting," she replies. "I shall drive you into the darkness once again." Her voice trembles, and I put my arm about her, and the words she does not say are *but only when I have to.*

The next morning we are gone, leaving Jalaino's dreams restful behind us, and Amorket to husband her loneliness, and me to bear mine until my feet carry me that way once more.

Acknowledgments

A huge thank-you to my agent, Simon, and to my editor, Lee, and everyone else at Tordotcom Publishing. Thanks also to everyone who enjoyed *The Expert System's Brother.*

About the Author

© Kate Eshelby

ADRIAN TCHAIKOVSKY is the author of the acclaimed Shadows of the Apt fantasy series and the epic science fiction blockbuster *Children of Time*. He has won the Arthur C. Clarke Award, a British Fantasy Award, and a British Science Fiction Association Award, and been nominated for the David Gemmell Legend Award and the Brave New Words Award. In civilian life he is a gamer and amateur entomologist. He was a full-time lawyer until recently, when he decided to write full time, instead.

TOR·COM

Science fiction. Fantasy. The universe.

And related subjects.

*

More than just a publisher's website, *Tor.com*
is a venue for **original fiction, comics,** and
discussion of the entire field of SF and fantasy,
in all media and from all sources. Visit our site
today—and join the conversation yourself.